1

Published by White Tea Studios.

www.whiteteastudios.com | info@whiteteastudios.com

Classification: (1) Magic Realism. (2) Thriller. (3) Paranormal.

This book is designed to entertain. It is sold with the understanding that the author or publisher is not engaged in rendering any professional advice. If such advice or assistance is required, the services of a competent professional should be sought out.

Credits

Cover and interior design: Yousuf Tilly. Additional
graphic elements: freepik.com, Wikipedia.com

This book is available at a discount for bulk
purchases in electronic, print or audio formats.

For further information,
email: info@whiteteastudios.com

For S, a man,

Y, the portal,

and A, my world.

KARMA CRIME

By Yousuf Tilly

Chapter One

The pen may be mightier than the sword, but the ear is smarter than the word. Silence. That was all Amina heard while watching her family chew through their dinner.

There and then, she decided that she was done with recipes. She was never going to write down another one, even though cooking shows were wildly entertaining. Popular television chefs often licked their fingers, pontificating about their methods being the most satisfying, but it all seemed like the performance of circus monkeys now. Amina wasn't interested in showing off anymore. It completely missed the point.

The roasted chicken and vegetables sitting humbly on the table was the real thing. It was a dish that epitomized normalcy, and neither did Amina add any finesse to it by using a fancy recipe. The silence around the dinner table that night confirmed that it wasn't a formula that made a good meal. It was serving people what they wanted to eat, in the way that they liked it.

Everyone, who was anyone, appreciated the care that went into a plate of mum's authentic home cooking.

Little Mo, for instance, had his lips wrapped around a spoonful of mushy peas. None of it had actually gone into his mouth. Instead, his cheeks were puffed up like a chimpanzee's while he aligned the green blob, and then sucked the mess in through his teeth. The squishy sound it made delighted him immensely. He, no doubt, was imagining himself as the gorilla on the packaging that the peas came in. Mo often aped it in a deep

Herculean voice and, to feed his imagination, Amina had ignored all advice on the perfect mushy peas and blitzed the poor things to smithereens. Admittedly, hers looked like vomit, but the glee on Mo's face was priceless.

Fatima frowned at Mo's savagery. It was a sign of disgust that would ordinarily be voiced, but she found talking with food in her mouth equally repugnant. It was quite a conflict to be suffering at her tender age, though Amina's daughter was pedantic about rules. She did everything methodically. For her, Amina made an especial effort to thicken her gravy so that it didn't run off into the other compartments on Fatima's plate. Fati, as she was affectionately called, had rather clinically separated the potatoes, meat and peas on her plate so that they wouldn't infect each other. She liked to savour each taste, one at a time. Amina liked to think of that quirk as a talent for gastronomy, and the semblance of order that the stiff gravy added to her little girl's world made Amina's heart skip a beat. All it took to make Fati happy was a pinch of culinary rebelliousness.

Unlike the children, their father ate with his hands. He handled his food the way he did all of life. A good grip, Anwar's father had taught him, was the only logical way to navigate uncertainty. Amina watched him chew all of the thirty-two times that his dentist advised was good for digestion. That too was a recipe, but mothers can't always be prescriptive while remaining the support behind everyone else. Families were bound together by embracing the uniqueness of its individual members, and that made Amina more inclined to go with the flow.

It was a change in her that happened in the strangest of ways.

While the first few years of Mo and Fati's lives were characterized by enthusiastic doting, the demands of parenthood later began feeling like an imposition. After years of dishes and laundry, and then some more dishes and laundry, Amina felt fit enough to relinquish her gym membership altogether. Instead of a nimble body, being strong came to mean conquering repetitive chores lest Amina rob herself of living her own life. Then, one night, Amina collapsed from exhaustion and found herself in a brothel, sharing a drink with a prostitute that looked uncannily like herself.

In the dream, Amina was man of service as he wore a uniform and hat to that effect. He ended up in a room where the prostitute peeled his clothes off for him. His arousal was apparent, and Amina felt what it may have been like for men to become erect. A salacious urge then overcame him as he watched the prostitute undress herself. They copulated on the bed without any intensity of emotion, except for the recurring visual of the man looking directly into the prostitute's wide-open eyes. It was a steady gaze, and even more captivating was the experience of Amina as a man who was enjoying a woman who looked just like her. When the man finally ejaculated, the warmth of their carnal juices mingled, and Amina felt pleasure from both sides of the gender divide. Of course, she understood that reality had confined her to a female's experience, but the dream was so poignant that it challenged Amina to look beyond her personal boundaries. She woke up with a new perspective toward many things, including food, which was as primal as sex.

Of course, every mother didn't have Amina's wild imagination, but one wasn't really necessary to appreciate the warmth of a dinner shared with family while the chill autumn winds howled outside on that ordinary Tuesday evening. A photograph may have been able to capture the tangibles of chicken, potatoes and peas, but it could never capture the silence between them. It was screaming the joy of motherhood that Amina felt within, and she simply went with the flow.

Her wandering thoughts were interrupted though when Mo kicked himself off his chair. Fatima took it as a cue, and placed her utensils neatly beside her plate before joining him. As kids do, they were expected to shuffle about before doing what they were about to do, but they didn't. They knew their places, and that made the whole charade all the more amusing to Amina. The rascals had thought this out.

What Amina wasn't expecting was for Mo and Fati to stand there like soldiers and thank her.

"For what?" Amina laughed, but her curiosity was piqued as the gesture felt strange.

She glanced at Anwar to see if he had a clue as to what the children were up to, but he continued emaciating a chicken drumstick unperturbed. It was only when Amina turned back to find the kids sheepishly seeking an answer from their father that she realized what was really going on.

Amina guessed that their father had told them she was sick, and they needed to help make her feel better. Those probably weren't Anwar's exact words, but Amina could imagine the conversation to have amounted to that. It was Anwar's style, diplomatic.

Still, appeasing their mother left the kids with confusion on their little faces.

Amina deliberately threw her arms wide open, and her children fell into them. It was hard to conceive of a hug being painful, yet the kids seemed relieved themselves to be over with the awkwardness. Children were too natural to be unloving, so hate had to be taught to them. Amina cringed inside and, before the moment became a lasting one, she sent them off to do their homework as usual.

She then settled down to finish her own dinner. It didn't taste the same. Then again, she was chewing on the possibility that the same silence she had perceived earlier as an unspoken joy could very well have been a looming discomfort. Was she that blind, she asked herself, or was she making up stories in her head?

Her doubts were amplified by Anwar, who behaved as if nothing had happened. In silence then, husband and wife sat across each other at the dining table. No words were really necessary. Amina was sick to the stomach anyway. The hurt had something do with her not saying what she was told to. She just knew it, and now she was definitely not going to do what was expected of her because having her children poisoned against her by her own husband was down-right disrespectful.

So much for the joy of motherhood. It left Amina in second place.

A day later, Anwar suddenly swerved the car off the road. The inventors of safety belts deserved credit for saving Amina's face from hitting the window, but they also strapped her in while being taken to an unknown destination down a dusty rural path.

"Why are you being so mean?" she yelled indignantly.

Anwar's grip remained firm on the steering wheel. He tossed her a stoic glance, but turned his attention back to the road without a word. It wasn't the only question he refused to answer.

When the kids didn't return home from school that afternoon at their usual time, Anwar skirted around their whereabouts by playing stupid. It was his way to disguise a lack of imagination at excuse, so Amina pacified herself by guessing that they were at their grandparents. His dismissive manner, however, still brought on a panic that finally exploded in the car. Amina wanted answers and, to get Anwar's attention, she yanked the handbrake lever up.

The wheels suddenly locked upon the gravel road, twisting the car sideways, and sending them skidding toward a sand embankment. Anwar shoved Amina back in her seat, and set the wheels free. Alas, it was too late to regain control of the car. It slid toward the barrier at a hellish speed and, in the dark night that surrounded them, two pairs of eyes glared brighter than the full moon in the sky above. Amina's fingernails were dug deeply into her seat as the embankment hurried to ram into them, but Anwar swiftly swung the steering wheel in the opposite direction, and the car luckily straightened out. They rolled to a stop, just barely kissing the embankment with the car's bumper.

Without a moment's notice, Anwar put his foot down again and raced ahead. Having completely ignored that Amina had almost killed the both of them was an omen that pointed to the emotional collision they found themselves in after what had happened. Whether their marriage could recover from it was a different matter, but the husband who Amina had spent the better part of her life with was now estranged to her, and yet another deafening silence ensued.

The car roared down the gravel road, deeper into the night. They had left the streetlights behind a long time ago, and the world had turned into a collage of sombre hues outside Amina's window. The rocky outcrops in the countryside cut jagged shapes into the canvas of the navy night sky and, as they sped through the menacing hills, first the farmstalls and then the rest of civilization dwindled. A sign reading 'Hekport' finally told Amina where they were headed to, but the headlights still only exposed that one dusty path that led yonder to God knows where. And then Anwar slammed the brakes. The car skidded to a stop, and they stood idling in the middle of nowhere.

There, Anwar scanned the dusty clouds billowing around them, apparently in search of something. A beam of light outside Amina's window spawned a portal in the blinding debris, and out of it emerged a ginormous hand that rapped its knuckles on her window.

Bang, Bang, Bang!

"Open the fucking window!" Anwar shouted at her, then slammed a button to roll it down himself.

The hand happened to be attached to an arm, at the end of which was a tall but elderly farmhand who was propped up by a wooden staff and tented over with rags. He shined his torch in Amina's face. Up close, Amina noticed that one of his eyes was defunct, and protruded from his skull like a purple grape. She gulped, and reached for Anwar's hand, but comfort wasn't on offer. Anwar was busy putting the car back into gear.

It was then that the dust clouds had settled, and Amina found themselves parked before a gate that kept a pack of vicious dogs at bay. The farmhand limped off to swing it open, yelling at the dogs to shut up, but they growled anyway.

Cruising through the gates, Amina quickly rolled her window up. A hound had leapt out toward her and, though she wasn't ordinarily disturbed by barking, she startled when the dog spoke to her in plain English. She shot a glance at Anwar, who seemed to have heard nothing, but Amina was sure that she didn't imagine the dog warning her to watch her back. For God's sake, no hound was that well-trained.

Get…a…grip, she sniggered to herself while approaching a farmhouse.

The ranch they had arrived at was the end of the road and, when Anwar shouted at her to simply 'come', Amina stepped out of the car willingly. All her life she wanted her man to lead, but never stopped to question where he would end up taking her.

The front door was swung open by a man wearing long white robes that made him look like a monolith. The beard growing out of his chin looked like a tree and, in a decidedly serious tone, the man explained that he was certain it would one day bear fruit. Given the bumpy ride there, Amina smirked at the quip, but nevertheless kept her guard up. Her reluctance did not go unnoticed.

Anwar, however, took the man's joke as wisdom and bowed his head respectfully. Perhaps he was trying to make an impression when taking the man's hand. It was meant for shaking, but Anwar cupped it in his palms. There were better ways to kiss someone's ass but, when Anwar addressed the man as Mevlana before any actual introductions were made, Amina suspected that they had met before.

Perhaps the dog was right, she thought.

Mevlana then stepped out of the doorway, and Amina and Anwar crossed the threshold into one of those turn of the century styled farmhouses. It was built entirely out of wood and stood upon a stone base. It sat bang-smack in the middle of a wide tract of barren land across which the autumn winds blew recklessly and attacked the gutters, trimmings and roof tiles. Inside, Amina could hear them clapping eerily away. It sounded as if there were a hundred souls gossiping about the couple who had just arrived, or at least were betting on whether Amina would sit next to Anwar on the settee. The father of her children was beginning to look like a regular creep that night, and the tension between them was at breaking point.

In the lounge, a younger woman sat cross-legged on the floor while grinding some herbs in a pastel and mortar. How she could see what she was doing mystified Amina as the only lamp burning in the room had been dimmed by a dark brown shade with little tassels hanging off the edge. It matched the colour of the walls, the drapery, the carpets, and the brown velour couch that was offered to Anwar and Amina to sit on. If not for an orange ornament sitting on the table beside, they could very well have been lounging in a carboard box. That the people were brown too made the whole scene even more ridiculous, but Amina kept an air of civility given the polite chit-chat about the home's history that Mevlana used to open the conversation.

"For many years this house was a sanctuary for the lost and confused," he began.

Amina frowned quizzically. She too was lost and confused as to what he meant. Mevlana explained that people visited what he called 'the home' when they were faced with problems that they couldn't solve.

"They don't come anymore?" she asked, noticing that he had used the past tense.

"Hekport has changed," Mevlana replied, "After the new road was built, people don't pass this outpost to travel between the provinces anymore, so the house fell into dilapidation."

"I would never have guessed," Amina retorted, quickly spotting the frayed carpets and paint peeling from the walls.

"Besides," Mevlana remarked in response to Amina's disdain, "many people don't believe in the power of spirit anymore."

Amina glanced at her husband, wondering why she had never detected his penchant for superstition before. She then remembered that no one can truly be known, and let it slide.

"Hmm, what do they believe in?" she finally asked.

"The power of money of course!" Mevlana chuckled, and his beard rustled along with the bounce in his belly.

"I can relate," Amina remarked. Anwar's new car was standing outside, and he was more careful with it than he was with her. "It's quite disappointing," she added.

"Well, why do you think you're here?" Mevlana asked.

"I don't know," Amina replied. "I'm a hostage."

Mevlana frowned, so Amina explained that she was led to believe that Anwar was taking her to fetch their children, and that too after much fussing.

"And then I ended up here," she concluded.

Anwar grunted disapprovingly. He was otherwise listening to the conversation with a sense of jubilance, but now began puffing through his nose like a dragon.

"So, what am I doing here?" Amina asked insolently.

"Someone cares about you obviously," Mevlana replied before Anwar could. Sitting on the edge of his seat, Anwar's body language seemed too abrasive for the game that Mevlana was playing with Amina.

"Love means different things to all of us," Amina snapped. She may have sounded disrespectful, but that was just how she felt.

"Hmm," Mevlana nodded, "let's just say that you're here to see another perspective."

Ah! Amina relaxed. She got the picture.

She was brought to this man to be fixed. Mevlana was some kind of mystic that helped people with problems that they couldn't solve themselves and, since Anwar's muscles and money weren't helpful in mending the dismal communication problem they were experiencing in their marriage, he was an ideal customer.

But there was nothing supernatural about what had happened. Amina had good reason for her actions.

She understood that Anwar did not agree with her response to the situation, but it wasn't his prerogative to decide for her. She had told him, and his family, that she would deal with it in the manner that she felt was fit. It angered Amina that Anwar had brought her to Mevlana as it implied that he assumed she was broken in some way. That was unkind.

Before she could sling her handbag on her shoulder and insist on being taken home, however, Mevlana's attention was suddenly diverted.

The woman sitting beside them on the floor loaded the herbs that she had been crushing into a little basin at the top of the orange ornament on the table. It turned out to be a type of diffuser that a match was held to. When the powdered herbs caught alight, Mevlana inspected the concoction with a handkerchief over his nose. He then held out his hand, and the woman put one half of a lemon in it. Mevlana pumped it to get the juices flowing, after which a few drops were squeezed over the burning embers. They expunged into a gassy cloud, and what remained in the diffuser were tiny bits of raw meat that cooked over the blazing herbs. Mevlana was satisfied by the distinct aroma of barbeque, and waved the thing away.

The woman then left the lounge with the little shards of meat in some tissue paper, and Amina heard the front door swing open. There was a loud whistle, after which a set of paws raced across the veranda's wooden floor. Thud! The sound of an animal's teeth gnashing drowned out as the front door was shut again. Khadija, as that's what Mevlana called the woman, then joined them again in the lounge. She placed the diffuser on the table between them which, by then, was oozing a steady wisp of blue smoke.

"Sniff it once," Mevlana said.

Amina laughed. "I will if he does," she exclaimed, turning to Anwar. "This is a couple's retreat with a twist isn't it?" she asked with a stupendous smile.

Mevlana searched Anwar's face for a response. He was chewing on his little finger, a habit that Amina knew much about. It indicated that Anwar was feeling anxious. Unlike him, Amina could stand on her own two feet, and they were gracious enough to walk her over to the water closet down the hall.

There, she shut the door calmly but spun around and fell back on it. A frantic heaving overcame her, and Amina cupped her mouth tightly to ensure that the panic wouldn't escape. A brave face had served her well, but the smoke she had refused to inhale still stung her eyes. In the mirror, she found that her mascara had run down her cheeks along with her tears. With her lipstick and hair still in place, it was a good look for a miserable tart, but Amina decided that no one could see her that way.

"Damn!" she cursed. She had forgotten her handbag in the lounge.

She found the bathroom drawer empty, but a few sheets of toilet paper were enough to clean herself up. Amina reached over to tear some off when a knock at the door startled her. Behind her, the door was already pushed ajar, and a hand offering a fresh towel had invaded her privacy. Amina recognized the floral print on the brown sleeve.

"You'll need this," Khadija's muffled voice said from behind the door.

"I'll use the tissue, thanks," Amina replied, but Khadija pushed the door open anyway and squeezed herself into the tiny bathroom.

"You're a guest!" Khadija shouted unnecessarily, and so Amina took the towel.

She was then pushed away from the basin so that Khadija could turn the hot water faucet on herself. The plumbing banged in the wall before water coughed out of the tap. Khadija tested the water with her fingers, and adjusted the temperature.

"Old houses y'know," she quipped.

Amina resumed her place at the sink, expecting to be left alone, but Khadija skirted around to the cupboard where she found a fresh bar of soap. She sat down on the toilet to unwrap it, and waited to find Amina's eyes in the mirror.

"That was courageous," Khadija said. Amina ignored her so Khadija clarified. "In there," she explained, nodding in the direction of the lounge.

"What do you mean?"

"Oh, you know!" Khadija teased, "standing up to your husband like that."

Amina refused to dignify that comment with a response. Instead she dropped her gaze into the basin where she dipped the edge of the towel into the hot water and began wiping her cheeks clean. In the mirror, Khadija rested against the toilet's cistern, staring dreamily at the floor. She was mumbling to herself, something about how men take liberties, then suddenly startled.

"What are you going to do?" Khadija asked, rather worrisome.

"About what?"

"He's not going to let you off so easily," Khadija replied.

"I can handle my husband, thank you very much," Amina retorted, rinsing her face in the mirror.

"I meant Mevlana," Khadija explained.

"Oh?"

"Husband's usually let him do whatever he wants," Khadija said, and then leaned in to hand Amina the bar of soap, "because he gets the job done."

Amina took it from her. She hadn't a clue what Khadija meant but wasn't planning on sticking around the old farmhouse to find out either. Actually, she was intending to return to the lounge with the threat of divorce if her husband didn't take her home, and to her children, immediately. But that wasn't Khadija's business.

"Well, I can't see how Mevlana gets anything done around here without you," Amina said, turning back to the basin to lather her hands.

Khadija was taken aback by that statement, and stared at Amina.

"These towels," Khadija cried, "who's going to wash the make-up off them? And this toilet…I've got to clean it every time. Even the stupid plumbing. I'm on my knees fixing the pipes," Khadija lamented, lifting her dress to show Amina her bruises.

"You've got to decide your own worth," Amina told her, "you're not a slave, are you?"

"Nooo!" Khadija sighed. The trouble however was that she was quite afraid that Mevlana may punish her if she didn't obey him. "What if he doesn't talk to me anymore?" Khadija asked.

"It sounds like you're killing yourself trying to satisfy him anyway," Amina quipped, and Khadija froze as if she had just received a revelation from God.

It was quite possible that Khadija hadn't even conceived of having a life of her own. To Amina's mind, Khadija was a victim of a culture that didn't respect individuality, and might have felt quite alone in that big farmhouse located in the middle of nowhere.

Like herself, Khadija probably hadn't been lent an ear of support in a long time.

"You and I are not so different after all," Amina told her, and Khadija's face instantly lit up.

She jumped off the toilet and grabbed the towel from Amina's hands. Khadija then patted Amina's neck dry and fixed her clothes. The invasion of personal space took Amina by surprise, and she was too late in stopping Khadija from pushing a bang of hair behind an ear. Once it was back in place, Khadija met Amina's astonishment in the mirror. Amina wasn't sure, but it looked like adoration in Khadija's eyes.

"That husband of yours is a lucky man," Khadija whispered.

"Please tell him that when we go back to the lounge," Amina quipped.

"I'd just stop screwing him!" Khadija exclaimed, "that'll set him straight!" It was so unexpected a comment that Amina laughed.

"Do you think that'll work?" Amina jested, but Khadija's brow knitted and her face turned serious.

"Do everything twice, that's what I say," she replied.

Then, in the strangest gesture that anyone had ever made for Amina, Khadija reached into her bra and pulled out a pack of cigarettes. It was squashed, and a little sweaty, but she took one out and laid it down on the counter along with a lighter.

"To calm the nerves," Khadija whispered with a broad smile across her face, as if she was doing something naughty. She then left the bathroom, and Amina to her own devices.

"People!" Amina grimaced to herself in the mirror. They just use you, she thought.

A few moments later, Amina was battle-ready again. Her face was stripped of make-up, but there was a resilience in her gaze. It was the real Amina staring back in the mirror, the same one that felt no guilty for who she was. She hopped out of the water closet and into the hallway cursing her love of surprises.

And then she suddenly got another!

On the wall across was hanging an old but curious sepia photograph. Amina stowed the cigarette and lighter in her pocket, and stepped closer to examine the picture-frame. It was taken on the stairs that led up to the front door of the farmhouse, and captured both Mevlana and Khadija standing alongside another woman. Amina hadn't met her, but they may have all been Amish in a previous life since all three figures in the picture wore long black cassocks. Amina quickly dismissed that theory though when noticing the beaded necklaces that hung from their necks. Attached to each was a different coloured pendant made from precious stones. Interestingly enough, the dog in the photograph was wearing one too, and it was the same pitch-black hound that warned Amina to watch her back at the gates.

Amina loved animals, but she had never seen a dog with such unusually long and prickly ears before. They stood to the side instead of upwards, and the mystery of the strange ears got her thinking about what breed it was. Since men are dogs, Amina's mind quickly hopped, skipped, and jumped to the question of Anwar's character too, and an unusual memory that was dated the morning of Leila's engagement sprang to mind…

"Don't bang the door!" Anwar whispered rather loudly.

"Get off my back!" his elder brother, Brad, screeched right back.

Amina was caught between them outside the main bedroom door in her father-in-law's house. It was at the end of the passage, a dead end so to speak, where Anwar stood mano-a-mano with Brad.

"Have some respect," Anwar whispered, "it's your father in there."

Brad laughed, "I'm his doctor, I know what he needs."

"Don't be prick!" Anwar yelled, then toned down to a whisper again, "Pa has cancer. We all have to come to terms with it."

"By giving up?" Brad whispered back at the volume of regular yelling.

"Oh! I know where this is going," Anwar rolled his eyes, then drawled, "you want the money to give him proper care."

"You're pretty keen to put him in a box!" Brand sneered. "Maybe it's you that has an eye on Pa's inheritance."

Before their altercation evolved into a full-blown war, the door to Pa's bedroom swung open. Ma stepped out into the hall and closed the door quietly behind her. Vexation became her when she turned around to face her sons.

"If anything is going to kill your father, it's having raised two idiots!"

Ma pinched Anwar's ear. "Now everyone's hurting at the thought of losing Pa," she told him, and then pointed a finger at Brad, "and no one is slacking in their efforts to help him recover."

Both Anwar and Brad dropped their heads in shame as Ma reminded them that it was Leila's engagement that day, and it wasn't the time to be fighting about money. Leila was, after all, Brad's daughter and Anwar's niece, and she deserved their full attention. Ma then hugged her sons.

"…This is not the time to be arguing about money," Amina whispered to herself back in the hallway of the farmhouse. She repeated the phrase to the dog in the photograph while pondering its significance.

If she remembered correctly, it was Anwar who then gave his brother a hand to shake. The gesture showed that Anwar was a sensible man, and that was one of the reasons why Amina had chosen to marry him in the first place. She knew that Anwar had integrity.

Amina decided to drop the idea of threatening Anwar with divorce in favour of simply reasoning with him. This was perhaps just one of those times when they were disconnected, and couldn't fathom each other. Hmm, that simple wisdom could mend their marriage.

Amina smiled at the hound in the photograph. It was fast becoming her best friend, and Amina didn't even know its name. She blew its image a kiss, and the dog in the photograph just as casually lifted its paw and blew one right back at her.

Thud! Amina leapt back and hit the bathroom door behind her.

Something was happening to her and, before she could perform a quick introspection, she was distracted by a muffled voice coming from within the wall. The words were incoherent sounds, but they reverberated rather strongly within her as she recognized the voice. Amina put her ear to the wall to glean who was trapped inside, but logic luckily reminded her that the wall separated her from the lounge where Anwar waited.

Amina crept down passage, and peeped around the edge to spy into lounge. The first thing she noticed was that her handbag was missing from the spot where she left it.

"If Amina doesn't sort herself out tonight, our marriage is over," Anwar was telling Mevlana while his hands flailed about.

"That's pretty hasty," Mevlana remarked from the recliner he was relaxing in. Anwar's hands dropped as he paused to think.

"No! No! No!" Amina's mind was yelling.

She hoped that Anwar wouldn't share what she asked him not to speak about. It was a matter of privacy, and her trust would be severely betrayed if he did.

"Let me tell you why she's really here," Anwar finally said, and Amina knew that she was now truly alone in that farmhouse.

Chapter Two

"Hide!" Mo shouted when the countdown began.

The kids scattered across the lawn. Some leapt behind the hedges in the garden, while others found a wall to conceal themselves. Mo ran right through the scullery door, and into the kitchen where he climbed into his mother's apron. Amina tousled his hair and covered him before peeping out of the window again where she too was engaged in yet another game of hide and seek.

Pa's house was full of people that afternoon. A marquee was pitched across the grass in the backyard, and a frantic effort to decorate it was underway. It was being supervised by Anwar's brother and his wife, as it was their eldest daughter's engagement party, and none were more conscious of appearances than them.

"Eww! Leila's engagement photos are going to look like they were taken at a bush party," Marcia squealed. Amina cringed too.

Anwar's brother and his wife had decided to attend the engagement party dressed in matching leopard skin outfits. He wore the print on his shirt, over white trousers, while she matched him with the identical pattern on her dress, and finished the ensemble with white shoes and a belt. Their outfits were embarrassing to say the least.

"How did you even…?" Marcia asked.

"I was just joking," Amina chuckled, "I didn't think he'd take my comment about looking like a team seriously."

"His wife is certainly obedient!" Marcia joked. "Which wife takes fashion advice from her husband?"

"They belong in 'People Magazine', like Brad and Angelina!" Ma teased from over their shoulders. Amina's mother-in-law had crept up behind them to see what they were gossiping about, and startled the pair.

"Hey, those names are likely to stick!" Marcia quickly observed.

It was true too, but Marcia was really trying to draw attention away from herself and Amina goofing off their kitchen duties during a very busy morning.

"You got away with it too," Ma remarked, pinching Amina's flustered cheek, "which is why I need you to welcome the guests when they arrive."

"I-I-I need time to arrange the sweetmeats tray," Amina argued, but Ma sold it to her.

"You're warm. It's what Leila needs today," Ma said, and Marcia nodded eagerly as if she too thought it a wonderful idea.

"You're such a Judas!" Amina exclaimed when Ma left. She pinched Marcia on the cheek, just as Ma had done to hers.

"What was I supposed to say?" Marcia laughed, "clearly Brad and Angelina over there aren't thinking clearly today."

"Those names are definitely going to stick!" Amina remarked.

As the bride's parents, it was actually Brad and Angelina's duty to welcome the Ebrahim's, but Amina suddenly found the pressure of entertaining Leila's in-laws weighing heavy upon her shoulders. So, smiling like caricatures, she and Anwar greeted the

Ebrahim's at the front door. Anwar unclasped his hands from behind his back and offered Mr Ebrahim a handshake as stiff as a whiskey shot, while Amina hugged the groom's two sisters as if she'd known them all her life. She then turned her charm on Mrs Ebrahim.

"That's a lovely scarf you're wearing," Amina sang.

She leaned in to hug Mrs Ebrahim when the hefty woman caught Amina by the shoulders, and aborted the curtsy.

"You're not wearing a scarf?" Mrs Ebrahim asked.

Amina's disbelief was apparent, and it took a moment before her pleasantries recovered. "Erm, not all of us do," she replied respectfully.

"But this is a holy occasion!" Mrs Ebrahim preached. Her daughters echoed the sentiment, nodding the way refugees do when accepting that their homes have been burnt.

"Erm, welcome!" Amina abruptly exclaimed. She then swung her arm to invite the Ebrahim's into Pa's home.

"Come!" Mrs Ebrahim bellowed, huffing as she herded her family into the house. Clearly, she called the shots in their family.

"Hmm, that was a good start," Amina whispered to Anwar as they navigated to the lounge and sat Leila's in-laws down.

It turned out to be the longest thirty minutes ever. Amina served the Ebrahim's lemonade, but they preferred tea. After she had a pot brewed in the kitchen, they thought it was weak. Every attempt she made to make the Ebrahim's comfortable in their home was met with criticism, and eventually Mrs Ebrahim shunned Amina in favour Anwar's company.

He was pretty good at issuing ooh's and ah's to carry a conversation that he had no clue about, but his lack of constructive replies prompted Mrs Ebrahim to test him.

"What a beautiful culture we have!" she pontificated. "So much significance in calling it a 'Meethu Mouru', don't you think?"

"Oh sure!" Amina jumped into the conversation ahead of Anwar. He was glad too as polite banter wasn't his forte.

Mrs Ebrahim's chin dropped in her hand. Of course, she agreed with Amina that the ritual of binding two souls in eternity wasn't just a romantic notion. It was sacrosanct, and calling it a 'Meethu Mouru' aptly described the experience of a love shared. After all, the term literally meant 'sweet mouth' in Gujarati. Mrs Ebrahim actively listened to Amina, nodding emphatically while pretending to be actually be listening, and as soon as Amina had finished talking, she swiftly turned back to Anwar.

"And do the men have a more practical perspective?" Mrs Ebrahim asked, feigning such interest that Anwar froze.

"Erm…" Anwar managed to eke out while unconsciously biting his crooked finger, and horrifying Mrs Ebrahim. He always did that when expectations got the better of him.

Amina only then realized what she'd dragged her poor husband into. She felt guilty for wielding the 'duty card' when Anwar complained that his little finger was a serious disability to any welcome party. Anwar was conscious of it ever since the accident in the gym that bent it askew, and it truly did elicit a frown when others noticed it. Amina empathized, but encouraged Anwar not to think too much of what other's thought about him. She sometimes pressed that button when the occasion called for it, and the news of Leila's future in-laws being, well, rather stiff demanded it.

To rescue Anwar from Mrs Ebrahim, Amina signalled him with an eyebrow wave, which he took a moment to read before startling, and then lowered a tray of treats for the groom to choose from. The boy was sitting ramrod-straight in a chair, and looking rather numb on his own big day.

"Don't spoil your appetite!" Mrs Ebrahim suddenly shouted.

Mr Ebrahim then blew his nose into a handkerchief so hard that Anwar and Amina decided to reconvene in the kitchen.

"People!" Amina vexed when they found some privacy.

"Let's kill them," Anwar replied deadpan.

Amina was so upset that she laughed. They both did, glad to be on each other's side. Their trust in each other however didn't solve the problem of helping the Ebrahim's enjoy themselves.

In the interest of time, it was decided that Amina and Anwar split up. Anwar grimaced while volunteering to keep the Ebrahim's occupied, but it was necessary for Amina to prepare the sweetmeats. They were an instrumental prop in the engagement ritual, and Ma was relying on Amina to make it special. Amina watched Anwar march off to the family frontlines with a sentimental heart. His chivalry was appreciated, and she resolved to return the kindness by putting nothing less than her best efforts into her kitchen duties.

She hoped that showing a sense of solidarity on Leila's big day would relieve some of the tension between Anwar and his brother. As

Leila's father, Brad would appreciate that.
Besides, Amina refused to allow the
Ebrahim's attempt at making her feel useless
interfere with that.

The kitchen however was in a mess and
Amina couldn't find a thing, least of all the
critically important pink box. She saw it arrive
that morning, but rummaging through the
cupboards proved to be a futile exercise.

"Marcia!" Amina yelled.

"It's right here," came a reply from the
scullery, and then Marcia emerged.

They shuffled over to the counter excitedly
where the box was laid down and the
cellophane tape ripped off the edges. Marcia
carefully lifted the lid.

"Wow!" they both gasped while peering into
it.

Their awe was interrupted by a knock on the window from Marcia's husband, Dawood, who needed some help. Marcia glanced at Amina, and was assured that Amina could handle things by herself.

"How long do you think it took them to make that?" Marcia asked.

"Definitely not the amount of time we have," Amina replied.

That set things into motion, and Amina snatched a knife from the drawer, but alas too quickly. It let slip and the knife's point almost drilled right into her hand. Marcia caught her before making another attempt, and eased the knife out Amina's hand.

"No pressure," she advised, then shouted, "coming!" when Dawood knocked on the window again. "Bye!" she waved, and shuttled out of the kitchen door.

Amina sat down for a minute. She picked up the knife again, this time with a steady grip, and scraped her thumb across the blade's edge. She certainly was a danger to herself when feeling this anxious.

Using the knife more consciously, she sliced off a piece of confectionary in the box and popped it into her mouth. The taste alone transported her to another place, and Amina shut her eyes to savour it. She often felt the need to just get away from it all, but the great tragedy of adulthood was a lack of time, and she was shaken by a little hand almost immediately thereafter.

"Mummy, are you dead?" her son Mo asked.

"Not anymore," Amina replied, opening her eyes.

The first thing Amina noticed were the scuff marks on her little boy's pants. Great! At least he would match Brad and Angelina's animal outfits in the engagement photos. Why his pants were tucked into his socks was also beyond Amina but, when Mo explained that they flapped when he ran, Amina refrained from scolding the boy. She was reminded of his innocence, and the simplicity of it inspired her.

"Please fetch me some flowers," she asked, pointing Mo to delicate lilies in the garden.

Mo ran off with the same chivalry that his father had shown earlier, and Amina watched her other favourite man in the world dive into the flowerbed at her behest. The scuff marks may have multiplied, but that was love.

Ma didn't say a thing when Amina showcased her handiwork a little later, but Amina knew her mother-in-law well enough to know when she had surpassed expectations. They were standing around a shiny blue tray on the counter that was both inviting and untouchable at the same time. It looked like an island paradise for lovers, and Ma complimented Amina's sweetmeat arrangement by asking how she could still, at this age, maintain such a sexual mind.

The lilies from the garden were carefully trimmed at different lengths, and their stems tied into a bouquet that stood in the centre of the tray. Their delicate leaves soared above a mountain of chocolate and cream marbled halwa chunks that were cut with angular edges to mimic a natural landscape. It was all bordered by light yellow meethai slices that drew a beach on the shiny blue decorative tray, and the encore was bite-sized cubes of minty-green pistachio barfi strategically loaded atop to express abundant vegetation. The confectionary island wasn't just a lover's paradise, it emulated the divine.

Barfi itself was a heavenly delicacy.

It was the most popular of all Indian confectionary, perhaps because it is neglect that breeds the need for significance in people. Neglect leaves something to be proved, which is our true natures that we are all in search of, but when lacking an understanding of who we truly are, it is impossible to define in what way we are significant. And that's what barfi does. It pacifies, like a mother's milk. In fact, three kinds of milks comprise its key ingredients. They are infused with cardamom, and release the fragrance when the smooth texture of curdled milk dissolves in the mouth. The nutty undertones of roasted pistachio then linger on the tongue while, in the tummy, a magical sensation that feels akin to being carried in a mother's womb returns like an old memory. Barfi reminds people of a time when love was so natural it was ordinary, and that is why barfi is the staple of all Meethu Mouru's, a ceremony in which something sacred is born.

Either that, or Amina was concocting another ridiculous story in her head.

Gee, if only she could steady her mind. Lately, it had been out of control. When she tuned back into reality, the idea of making a grand entrance of the sweetmeats tray had struck. If anything could impress the Ebrahim's, Ma said, it was probably their best bet.

Amina and Ma imagined it out loud.

Everyone would already be seated in the marquee after lunch, except of course the smokers. Leila and the groom would then be asked to take the occasional chairs at centre stage. As an aside, Amina and Ma both agreed that the big oriental rug, pot plants and drapery was an exotic enough setting for the ceremony. Mrs Ebrahim and Leila's mother, Angelina, would kick things off with an embrace. Once the formal approval of marriage by the 'heads of familia' was out of the way, Leila and her beau would then become the focus of all attention. That was when Amina would be given the signal to come and unveil the tray of sweetmeats. Ta da! The rest was easy to work through. Mrs Ebrahim would then feed Leila some sweetmeats, and Angelina would get her turn to do the same to the groom thereafter.

Ma and Amina glanced at each other. If everything went as expected, as tradition would have it, the Ebrahim's would be happy, and this gesture would be a generous one for Leila. After all, Leila was going to the spend the rest of her life with the Ebrahim's.

"I hope you saved the best sweetmeats for later?" Ma asked, glancing at the sweetmeat island once again.

"Of course I did," Amina quipped, "only the worst ones are on the tray."

Playfulness remained in the kitchen after Ma left.

Mo had found a cricket in the flowerbed that remained hidden in his pocket until he decided, as kids do, that it was hungry. Actually, he was itching to taste the barfi himself while using the poor insect as an excuse, but when Mo opened his hands to show it to his mother though, the cricket sprang away. Little Mo began wailing and, trying to avoid disturbing the guests in the marquee, Amina found herself chasing a cricket in high heels. She eventually cornered it in a cupboard and handed it back to Mo. Like magic, a smile appeared on his face, and she melted. She picked off a cube of barfi from the tray and gave it to Mo. At least it would keep him busy while she fixed herself up again.

Amina worked speedily to pin her hair back into place, and tie her sari tightly again. She didn't wear traditional clothing often, and it was no cinch to roll herself back into the train of chiffon that made the skirt and bodice of her sari. One eye, of course, still peeled out the window waiting for Ma's signal, which came all too quickly. Ignoring the state of her make-up, Amina grabbed the tray of sweetmeats on her way through the kitchen door.

An applause erupted when Amina arrived in the marquee.

Mrs Ebrahim and Angelina were satisfied that a suitable impression was made on the guests, and embraced each other to signify the joining of souls, bloodlines and fortunes. Of course, they had both done ample homework into each other's families before agreeing to betroth their children to each other, so the actual engagement ritual was just a formality. Amina passed the tray over to Ma and, when the whole shindig began, she stepped back to watch from afar. Finally, she could relax.

She found Anwar standing against a wall, glad that the Ebrahim's were off his hands. Amina tangled herself in Anwar's arm and drew herself closer to him. She lifted herself onto her tiptoes and lightly nibbled his nose. It was gratitude for standing by her side, and he responded with a mutual nip on her snout. It was their thing.

By then, Mrs Ebrahim had just finished feeding Leila a piece of halwa. Angelina then got her turn to put a slice of meethai in the groom's mouth. She then followed with a cube of barfi, and then another, and then another. Everyone laughed. Stuffing the poor boy's face while he wasn't expecting it was rather funny. He couldn't even chew let alone ask Angelina to stop, and Mrs Ebrahim planted her hands on her hips in annoyance. But it was clean fun, and everyone cheered Angelina on.

Suddenly there was violent lurching, and the groom went blue.

His choking gave Angelina a fright, but not nearly as severe as the shock that overcame Mrs Ebrahim when Ma quickly swung around to the back of the groom's chair. Ma pushed him forward and pounded her hand on his back. A huge mess of green barfi hurtled out of his mouth and landed right on Mrs Ebrahim's shoe. While he was relieved to be alive, a great gasp echoed through the marquee.

Mrs Ebrahim dropped her gaze to her feet, and kicked the half-chewed lump of barfi off her toe. There amidst the debris, was lying the bitten carcass of an insect oozing a green goo.

The groom's sisters were mortified, and covered their mouths while Mrs Ebrahim suffered a dizzy spell before feinting in the pot plants. Leila burst into tears, so her mother cradled her, and Ma herself was in disbelief.

The marquee fell silent as all eyes turned on Amina. This was her handiwork, they all knew. She had taken the credit for it, after all, when proudly displaying the sweetmeats.

Amina's face gave her away. The reasons for the disaster were written all over her but, with so much anger directed at her, Amina also knew that she couldn't tell a living soul about how that insect ended up in the groom's mouth. There was just too much at stake so, in the dreaded silence that followed, Amina burst out laughing, and continued to laugh, and laugh until tears flowed from her eyes.

"Who does that?" Anwar asked, throwing his arms up.

It was how he concluded the tale of why he had brought Amina to Hekport. Relating the incident to Mevlana back at the ranch still left him as clueless as the countless times he badgered Amina for answers.

Why did she laugh?

The mystic scratched his beard while thinking the happening over. Amina crossed her arms and refused to comment, just as she had when initially interrogated about the stray cricket, and that was really at the heart of Anwar's frustration with Amina.

"She's been falling apart like that lately. Doing things…things!" Anwar yelled, his arms flailing about again. It was a rather large accusation he was making, and Mevlana asked him to elaborate.

"They're like episodes," Anwar replied, "lapses of judgement in which Amina doesn't know what she's doing…"

Anwar stopped short of finishing his sentence and fell into a pensive mood. Everyone watched him chew his crooked little finger while the cogs in his mind turned, and then he whispered, "…or does she know what she's doing?"

Amina flinched at his doubt in her.

She had played Anwar's account of what had happened at the engagement in her head while he related it, and even agreed as to its accuracy, but the narrative ended differently in their respective minds. She searched her own memory to decipher how he had come to the conclusion that she was suffering episodes, and it was a conversation that transpired on the morning of the engagement that helped her understand why…

The curtains in the spare room in Pa's house were drawn, and Anwar was cladding himself in a suit while Amina wrapped herself into a dusty pink sari. Neither of them could remember the groom's name.

"No one lets him talk," Amina observed.

"He's young. Maybe his family doesn't trust him yet?"

"Well they must love him?" Amina asked, "he's their child."

"Well what will you say if Mo arrived one day on a motorcycle with tattoos on his chest and a needle in his arm?" Anwar said. He was pushing her to think little deeper, and Amina did.

"Hmm, I don't know," Amina finally replied, "I'd have to wait and see."

"Exactly!" Anwar exclaimed. "You won't know what to do until it happens. Only then will you be able to gauge how your son's actions will impact your life."

"Tsk, I'm his mother!" she retorted. "I'll impact him!"

"Don't assume that he needs your help. Maybe that's his choice."

"Parenthood!" Amina remarked while hooking an earring in.

"Yeah," Anwar mumbled, "so much for wanting the best for those you love…"

Those words continued ringing in Amina's mind as her attention returned to the couch she was sitting on in the farmhouse.

Anwar knew the meaning of those words intimately. His father, Pa, was a lovely man, but was also a patriarch that ruled their family with an iron fist. Anwar often felt like he had missed the opportunity to become his own man, and Amina's guess was that he spent the amount of time he did in the gym as a means to toughen up. But Anwar was also his father's child. In their marriage, Anwar liked to exert control too, and routinely excused force as wanting to do what was best for those whom he loved.

Such a bully would probably be offended by being disagreed with, and it made sense to Amina as to why he was accusing her of having 'episodes'. She acknowledged his sincerity but, all in all, was left in a rather precarious position.

She was honestly struggling with the repercussions of her infamous guffaw at the engagement party, but Mevlana's assistance came at the cost of admitting to what really happened. Handling the situation by herself was a much better idea. Amina managed to stave everyone off by promising to talk about it when she was good and ready, but that hadn't been working out well thus far either.

It really was a question as to whether she should place her trust in others or herself?

Before she could make up her mind though, Anwar continued his tirade.

"She said it was care by restraint. What the fuck does that mean? …care by restraint!" Anwar cried. To him, it seemed that Amina was expecting everyone to simply drop the rather serious matter and continue as if nothing had happened.

"It sounds like manipulation to me!" Anwar shouted angrily, or rather, helplessly.

"What if she doesn't want your help?" Khadija suddenly interjected.

Mevlana's eyes popped. He sat forward in his seat and promptly backhanded her. Khadija went flying into Amina, who startled, but composed herself while Khadija nursed her face. Anwar addressed the question anyway.

"No!" he grimaced. "This is a can of worms. My relationship with my brother is…is already difficult, and now his kids won't associate with mine." The consequences of Amina's behaviour were tearing their family apart, and Anwar refused to stand for it.

"Amina is trying very hard to throw everything that she has away, including me and the kids, and she just won't say why."

Amina's mind short-circuited. Guilt usually tripped her up that way. The dim bubble of light they were sitting in suddenly skewed her perception. It reflected only sporadic parts of the scene, like some staccato impression of reality. Anwar's nose, Mevlana's hand, and a wisp of Khadija's hair painted a cubist rendition of reality in her mind. Before

Amina's very eyes, the walls receded into the shadows and the floor gave way. They seemed to be floating upon an endless abyss, and Khadija was staring at Amina as if none of it was imagined.

"Why won't you say anything?" Mevlana asked again when Amina didn't respond the first time.

Amina continued staring at the mystic, dumbfounded. Her answer was clearly articulated in her mind, but her mouth wouldn't reciprocate. She dropped her gaze instead.

"Can you see how good she is at this?" Anwar exclaimed. "That silence is a distance from here to kingdom come. She told me to trust her. That she'll handle it in the way she needs to, but what she really means is to stop bothering her."

"Well, why are you so bothered?" Mevlana asked, directing Anwar to the point of his rant. Anwar sighed, and hung upon himself.

"Because I'm the father of our children and I want to protect us all." Anwar replied, and then paused to hide the crack in his voice. He was almost in tears when he said, "I do love you Amina, but you're asking me to be someone I'm not."

"Well then, let's see the nature of your love," Mevlana exclaimed.

His beard jerked wildly as he threw his arm out to point somewhere. Khadija sprang up from the floor, and momentarily disappeared. After some shuffling in the back of the lounge, she materialized again with a book. It was huge, and had a copper clasp keeping it shut. The ancient grimoire was handed respectfully over to Mevlana.

A secret was whispered to it, and the clasp snapped open. Mevlana paged through the great book to find a spell that made him smile. He read the words in a foreign tongue, and then slammed the book shut before shaking it violently over the table. Miraculously, iron filings rained from it, and spread themselves across the table.

The mystic then grabbed Anwar by the wrist. He flattened Anwar's fingers and waved the palm across the filings. Amina was asked to do the same, which she reluctantly did, but it turned out to be a pointless exercise as nothing happened.

"When two likes' come together, two people who are similar," Mevlana said, "then they see themselves in each other. They can create immense love between them, but such a deep devotion can also drive them to fall in love with an idea rather than each other."

Mevlana picked up the grimoire again and passed it down the length and breadth of the table. As he did so, the smattering of iron filings danced and reformed themselves as two distinct groups on either end of the table, as if they were charged by a magnet.

"Yours is clearly a case of opposite energies attracting each other," he said, glancing at Anwar and Amina in turn. "You complement each other wonderfully," Mevlana smiled before his face turned grim, "but if you're not careful, it's easy to get competitive with each other, and then ridicule will destroy the both of you."

Anwar and Amina glanced at each other guiltily.

They were both eager to hear Mevlana's proposal on how to reconcile their differences. Before he could do so, though, he needed to decipher the nature of the episodes that Amina was experiencing. Thereafter, it was their choice to decide on how to go forward.

"Do I have your permission?" Mevlana asked Amina.

She was about to ask what she was giving permission for when Anwar interrupted.

"If you want to see the kids again, then say yes," Anwar warned, "before tonight ends, this ends!"

Ouch! That was insensitive. Anwar knew that Amina would do anything for her kids. She hated him in that moment, but nodded in the affirmative anyway. What else could she do?

The orange diffuser was lit once again, and the powdered herbs within crackled as they did before. Soon a wisp of blue smoke rose into the air, and Khadija offered the concoction to Amina. This time, she inhaled deeply. The smoke stung her nose, and Amina's face squashed. In her mind, she justified slighting herself with all kinds of reasons, but none of them mattered when she opened her eyes again. Amina herself couldn't believe it...

She was invisible.

Chapter Three

The tub of ice cream sweated patiently on the table. Mo and Fatima sat quietly for a change, their eyes glazed over as Ma waved a spoon before them. It was a cunning plan that Ma had. With any luck, the children would be hypnotized enough by the possibility of enjoying a bowl of the chocolate desert and, in exchange, Ma would find the answers she was looking for.

"You never tell me how much you love me," she began, "and I want to know!" The blank looks on their faces accosted Ma, so she put a smidgen of space between her thumb and forefinger to proffer an answer. "This much?" she asked.

Mo smirked, thinking it a silly game. He nudged his sister, but Fatima was like her mother and considered the question first.

"Do you love me as much you love ice-cream?" Ma asked Fati, nudging her playfully too. Monkeying Mo managed to elicit a smile from her granddaughter, but that was it. Neither Mo nor Fati had taken the bait.

"Hmm!" Ma sighed. "If you don't love me then I think I'll put this ice-cream away," she feigned seriousness.

"No!" Mo exclaimed. He promptly flung his little arms wide open when Ma asked again how much he loved her. "This much!" he yelled, and Ma pried open the lid of the ice-cream tub to tease him.

He was rewarded with a scoop of chocolate ice-cream, and Fatima instantly saw the game for what it was. She leapt off the sofa and ran all the way to the wall and back.

"I love you that much!" she exclaimed, slapping her hand on the sofa. It earned her two scoops in a bowl.

"She's got more!" Mo complained, his own lips still dripping with chocolate.

"If you tell me what happened at home, I'll give you another," Ma bargained with him.

Mo didn't even hear her. By the time Ma finished her sentence, his little legs had carried him out the living room.

"This much!" he yelled from somewhere down the passage and, when Mo returned, expecting to see another scoop of ice-cream in his bowl, a competitive spirit had overcome the children.

Not to be outdone, Fatima shouted that she loved Ma more than the whole wide world, and the siblings continued bickering until Ma was loved as much as the galaxy, solar system, and universe.

Ma sighed. There was no reasoning with those children when they were so excitable. She let her inquiry go unanswered while dishing out another scoop of ice cream for each. She hoped that a generous bribe would twist their little arms into telling her what she needed to know.

Anwar had arrived unexpectedly that afternoon to drop them off, which was unusual to begin with, and then abruptly excused himself and Amina for having an appointment later that evening. Before Ma could ask what time he'd be back to fetch the kids, Anwar was gone. Ma patiently helped the children finish their homework, eat their dinner, and put their pyjamas on, all the while wondering why they seemed to be in a such strange mood.

With the kids at their grandparents, and Anwar and Amina gone missing, Ma was certain something was going on at their home. She just didn't have a clue as to what.

"Playing the devil's advocate, were you?" Pa chuckled when Ma left the kids to their treat and joined him on the couch.

He wasn't pleased though that Ma had riled them up so. Their yelling had completely destroyed his peace. The medication he took for his cancer had left him feeling woozy, and now there was no way he could sleep it off. With Ma, Pa watched the kids losing their minds, and wished that a bowl of ice-cream could solve adult troubles too.

The Ebrahim's had demanded an inquest into the debacle at the engagement ceremony, and held Leila's marriage to their son hostage until they received a satisfactory explanation. It was silly of them really, but everyone was now looking to Pa and Ma to rescue Leila's marriage. How could they when neither Ma nor Pa knew whether the groom swallowing an insect was an accident or not?

"Anwar has been pushing Amina pretty hard about it," Ma said.

"It's a much bigger thing for him," Pa said, "y'know, while Anwar and his brother are fighting the way they are."

"That's your fault!" Ma exclaimed, "you should've said something to those boys."

"Ya-ya! …and now it's out of control," Pa finished her thought for her. It was an appeal actually, to not start that discussion with him right then.

"The whole family is under pressure," Ma continued anyway, "they feel like they have to choose between Anwar and Brad."

"Oh, ignore what everyone says! They're just hedging their bets," Pa argued, "Everyone always sides with the guy who gets the money."

"It's still tearing this family apart," Ma replied.

"I built this family!" Pa cried so emphatically that he coughed. His chest wheezed while reassuring Ma that nothing would go wrong. It was just a matter of time before things settled again.

"There isn't any time left!" Ma yelled, but then restrained herself as a tear welled-up in her eye.

Pa softened, and put his arm around her. It was difficult for him to face his own mortality too. Realistically, everyone had to go sometime. It was just a fact.

Pa's imminent demise however was a problem looming over their household and, before Pa or Ma could rescue Leila's marriage, some housekeeping was in order. Ma wasn't concerned about financial trouble, but she did want to spend the time she had left with Pa in peace rather than in negotiations.

"Can't Anwar and Brad just split the money?" she asked in desperation.

"A 'waarso' is more than just money," Pa replied, "you know that."

"All I know is that the stupid tradition is making enemies of brothers!" Ma grimaced.

"It's tradition for a reason!" Pa exclaimed. "Someone has to take over the reins and lead the family. Together they can accomplish more than acting by themselves."

As head of the family, he knew that the tradition of 'waarso' itself didn't just mean doling out an inheritance. It implied an entire heritage, so an heir was someone who was also bequeathed Pa's authority over the family. The family patriarch was seen as almost godly, and the trouble between Pa's sons was then much more complicated than it looked. It could not be dismissed as an antiquated culture since entire lives and legacies were at stake. That required a sense of responsibility, and the best heir to a 'waarso' was a humble one.

"Well, Anwar is…" Ma said, choosing her words carefully, "a good man."

"Do you think he's lacking in leadership quality?" Pa asked.

"He's my son, but I saw his face when it happened," she remarked, "Anwar blames Amina for ruining Leila's engagement."

"Maybe she was at fault?" Pa wondered.

"Never!" Ma exclaimed. "Amina is nothing like that. Her standing at her husband's side during this whole inheritance fight says that she values family. Leila is family, so Amina wouldn't do something like that."

"Amina's not as innocent…," Pa replied but stopped prematurely. It was too late though to curtail his thought.

"…as she looks?" Ma asked.

Her intuition told Ma that Pa knew something she didn't. Ma pushed him to connect the dots in her mind. She already knew Anwar was adamant that he would lead the family far better than Brad ever could.

"Yes, he's arrogant!" Pa cried.

Ma noted the disappointment in Pa's voice and caressed his hand, but then her eyes opened to a cunning possibility. Anwar had lost all respect for his elder brother while feuding over the inheritance and it wouldn't come as a surprise if Anwar tried to gain the upper hand somehow.

"Wait! Are you saying that Anwar forced Amina hand to put the insect in the sweetmeats tray and ruin the engagement?" she asked.

Chapter Four

The puff of smoke lingered desperately in the air. It certainly had the potential to take shape, any shape, and then it may have instigated Amina's imagination just as clouds did when being watched on lazy days. But the wind blew across the veranda, and the smoke was abducted, taken away somewhere in the dark night. Amina took another puff of the cigarette. She was rocking gently on an old swing, wondering where billows of smoke really went to when they vanished. Everything seemed so mysterious to her.

"So, basically you're asking me to prove myself," she remarked, "only people do stupid things like that!"

Bruno raised his hind leg to scratch his ear. He was sitting on the swing with her, and its gentle rocking made his tail sway. "Well we are what we prove ourselves to be, don't you think?" he replied.

"Rubbish!" Amina said crossly, "labels only mean what you want them to."

"All I'm saying is that what we do defines us," Bruno said, raising an ear at Amina's unnecessary defensiveness. At the rate she was puffing the cigarette, it would hardly relax her.

"Okay," Amina said, turning to Bruno. "So why did you warn me to watch my back at the gates?"

"For exactly this reason!" Bruno exclaimed, pointing his paw at her. "Look at you, you're as high as a kite!"

"Prove it!" Amina instantly retorted, and they both realized that the conversation had gone full circle. Only people did stupid things like ask others to prove themselves.

That thought warranted another puff of the cigarette, and Amina furiously took one. To the naked eye, they were just a woman and a dog gently rocking away on a swing one moody night but, really, their conversation had all the charm of a domestic squabble. Being a dog who found it difficult to just let things go, Bruno leapt off the swing and thud upon the wooden veranda. He swung around to face Amina.

"How can you be invisible if we're having this conversation?" he asked.

"Maybe you're mad!"

"I'm a dog," Bruno replied, rolling his eyes, "dogs don't suffer mental disease."

"Have you ever heard the phrase 'mad dog'?" Amina sneered.

"I think you're missing the point," Bruno said, making another attempt to talk some sense into Amina. "A sniff of that concoction has made you high, and you don't even know it!"

A healthy suspicion overcame Amina. She stared pensively into the darkened field that surrounded the farm. Had there been any answers out there, she was determined to find them. Her confusion compelled her to, and she took another draw of the cigarette to steady herself. Perhaps Bruno was right. She certainly felt intoxicated when the image of her two beautiful children suddenly manifested in the night sky.

They danced, performing the same shenanigans that they used to entertain themselves when avoiding going to bed early. The delusion lightened Amina's mood as she realized that, even though the umbilical cord was cut at their births, she was still tethered to those children through the ether. Doing something for them remained the equivalent of affecting herself. Motherhood was the only true human connection she knew, and that was why Amina's children were about the only human beings she didn't dislike. She even allowed them to tell her what to do.

But then Amina heard her own mother's voice booming across the darkened field. It scolded her for making her children suffer for her stubbornness. Amina hadn't considered them when deciding to handle the conflict that followed Leila's engagement with tight lips.

The criticism left Amina with a gaping void within, into which doubt quickly filled, and she was soon asking herself if mothers even knew for sure whether their children loved them back. Mothers loved anyway, she convinced herself, successfully enraging herself for no reason whatsoever. Amina took another drag of the cigarette, and that's when it struck her that the only way to dispel her haunting thoughts was to employ her own doubt. It was, after all, simply an acknowledgement that she didn't know. That wasn't so bad.

And suddenly she saw a way out.

People routinely took advantage of her softer nature, and she was sick of it. That was really what bothered Amina. It was her own doubt that crippled her, and it was over her dead body that she would allow her children to suffer because of it. The only way to safeguard their innocence was make sure it was never risked again, and for that she had to destroy Anwar. Even a father didn't have the right to stand between a mother and her children. If Anwar thought that taking them hostage would sway Amina to do what he wanted, he had another thing coming. Between her children and her husband, there was no contest.

"Then will you forgive him?" Bruno asked.

He hadn't magically read Amina's thoughts. Bruno told her that she had been speaking out loud all along. While he thought that the absurdity of her talking to herself proved that she was out of her mind, Amina pointed out that it was much stranger to be entertaining a conversation with a dog.

"Who knows?" Amina replied, ignoring her embarrassment, and flicking the cigarette butt over the banister. "Besides, you should be happy. Forgiving Anwar will prove that I'm actually visible."

The windy night then refused stand still, and carried away with it the apparitions of

Amina's beloved children. Amina sighed, reminding herself that everything was exactly as it was.

And while she continued swinging in that murky night, Anwar watched her through the kitchen window. Amina looked like the star of a motion picture that he had seen one too many times. The characters were familiar, and Anwar had his favourite scenes, but the magic of the story had lost its grip on him. Now his wife looked like a starlet that he once had a crush on, still picture perfect, but inimitably distant in the same way that an audience can only watch a movie rather than engage with it. Amina was a lifetime away and, with the kitchen window between them, Anwar began to see the futility of thinking that movies were anything more than just stories. Being in love with the idea of someone wasn't quite the real thing, and he felt excluded from the very life he had built with Amina.

"I didn't even know she smoked," Anwar said when Khadija arrived.

"I don't see a cigarette in her hand!" Khadija frowned while peeping out the window.

Anwar shook his head. He didn't know whether to laugh or cry. "You only think you know someone…" he brooded.

"Well I like her," Khadija remarked.

"That's because you don't know her."

"You've just told me that we only think we know people!" Khadija retorted, "so how sure are you that you know her?"

Anwar turned to Khadija. Her comment stuck a cord.

Lately, when he was with Amina they fought, and when apart, they managed to continue screaming at each other through telephones. It seemed that the only thing he and Amina knew about each other was that they hated each other. For the first time he realized that a vast distance had grown between them.

A guilty cloud poured over Anwar as he wondered if he had been so distracted by his feud with Brad, or so distraught at the thought of losing his father, that he'd completely neglected Amina. Of course, it was also worth considering if the things that he and Amina had done to each other had forced them to grow in different ways. Even if distance was an occupational hazard of marriage, Anwar had no idea how to close the gap between them.

"Go to her," Khadija encouraged. The doorway was right there, but Anwar didn't move a muscle.

"Aww! Don't be a paw-paw face now!" Khadija teased.

Anwar was clearly afraid, so Khadija sent him off to Mevlana. She was instructed to do so as there still was work to do if Mevlana was to ease Amina out of her episodes. Whether Amina responded to any treatment was really her choice, and while that may reveal who Amina truly was, Anwar remained convinced that she was just one damn stubborn woman.

Khadija remained in the kitchen to find a pot. She filled it with water and slammed it onto the stove. Her cheek still seared from the slap that Mevlana gave her, and Khadija didn't just look like an elephant, she had the memory of one too.

In the scullery, she picked out the ingredients for the potion that Mevlana wanted brewed. They were carried over to the kitchen table where she chopped and sliced them. Into the pot of water was tossed a pair of frog's legs, eight spider eyes, two fresh cloves and some lemongrass. Lastly, she added a scoop of sugar. The recipe in the grimoire didn't call for it, but Mevlana said it was necessary that the brew tasted good. Though tempted to ignore his instructions, another slap on the face Khadija didn't want.

With a great big heave, she mustered up all the insolence she could find and spat it into the pot. That concluded the list of ingredients called for by the recipe, and Khadija covered the pot with a lid. When she turned the dial on the stove, the gas hissed, and a spark set it on fire. Soon the diabolical potion began brewing.

Outside the window, Amina and Bruno were still rocking on the swing. When its momentum pulled them toward the dark night, Amina disappeared momentarily, and when it swung back into the porch light, there she was again. Khadija spied on Amina as intently as Anwar did. She too was intrigued by who the woman really was.

To her, Amina tallied up to yet another frivolous housewife. Amina was wearing a pantsuit with a frilly blouse, and the outfit was garnished with her long black hair that hung straight down her back. She looked like someone in a department store catalogue, and Khadija hated the type. They were just too normal for her tastes. Amina, however, represented a possibility. She seemed a living example of something that Khadija couldn't quite put her finger on, but was responding to nevertheless, and that fascinated Khadija.

Consumed by the daydream of who she may become, Khadija didn't hear the pot boiling over. Only after the steamy tonic crept over the pot's rim and singed on the stove, did she get a shock. Khadija doused the flame with a wet cloth, and lifted the lid on the pot to allow the steam to escape. The potion simmered down, and Khadija watched the furious bubbles dwindle. Cutting the gas, she found that the potion had brewed perfectly. It looked just like water.

To test it, Khadija dipped a ladle into pot and blew on it lightly to cool the liquid down. She then poured a sample of it into the bottle that fed the rats. They were obviously thirsty in their cage, and fought their way to the spout for a drink. The winner pattered through the skirmish on its little feet and sucked greedily. Glug, glug! Once satisfied, it fell to its feet again. Almost instantly, the rat's little legs caved in. It lay there helpless while the other rodents scattered in the opposite direction. Their lame brother then closed its eyes and died.

"Some guys have all the luck…" Khadija sang.

It was a song she had heard a long time ago but it stuck with her for some reason. She chucked a handful of lily leaves into the pot and stirred the potion to help them infuse. The recipe said that they would knock the edge off the potion.

An awful grinding suddenly caught Khadija's attention. In the garden outside, Amina was yanking the starter cord of their lawnmower rather desperately. The motor turned, but she wasn't pulling hard enough to actually start the engine, and began yelling like a drunkard. Bruno hopped around while Amina pushed, prod, and kicked the mower. None of it helped to get the mower started either. While scolding Bruno for wagging his tail, as it really wasn't polite to laugh at others, Amina climbed into the seat of the lawnmower to gain some control.

Khadija giggled. A whiff of those herbs had really set Amina off, and Khadija considered taking them herself just for kicks. With her hand on her cheek, she wished that she could let herself loose too. One day, Khadija thought, she may just turn around and slap Mevlana right back.

That same insolent demon that stoked Khadija's anger reared its ugly head outside in the garden. To Amina, it was a familiar one. It climbed into her mind and exploded into a fog that waylaid even her best efforts to escape the farm.

She was manic, yet planned to ride the mower all the way back up the dusty path and to the main road where she could hitchhike to Pa's house. Once there, she would ask them to buy Anwar one of those double-horned hats that Napoleon Bonaparte is famous for wearing. The benefit of decorating tyrants was that ordinary people like herself could identify them, and when everyone had come to know Anwar for the control-freak that he was, his chances at claiming Pa's inheritance would be at an end. That'll show him. Destroying Anwar was all that Amina could think about. Once she did, he would know how she felt.

Relentlessly, Amina pulled the starter cord of the lawnmower over and over again as hard as she could, but to no avail.

"Stupid! Stupid! Stupid!" she cussed at the machine between her legs.

From the kitchen window where Khadija was watching, it all looked rather hilarious, but she could not have guessed that Amina was really cursing herself. Amina refused to give up on that stubborn lawnmower, and huffed and puffed until the demonic fog in her head suddenly gained the colour and definition of the night that she graduated…

"My daughter!" her Dad exclaimed while proudly placing Amina's graduation hat on her head.

Amina pushed it askew to tease him, and everyone chuckled. They were at a restaurant to celebrate Amina's newly acquired pharmaceutical degree, and her parents had invited Amina's uncle and aunt to share in the occasion. Each had pitched in to buy Amina a gift that she truly wanted, and it was presented to her in a little box that was tied in ribbons.

"D-aaaad!" Amina squealed when opening the box. She threw her arms around him. It was a key, and outside on the street was parked the car that it started.

Dad gulped his emotions down while wishing Amina a prosperous future. He had always been Amina's biggest fan, encouraging her to be independent and free. The car was his idea since he saw it as a way to mobilize her. She now had the means to establish herself in the world, and the key in her hand was a symbol of Amina's future.

Suddenly a world of possibilities was open to Amina.

Of course, Amina's mind was filled with adventure. She dreamt of using her car to drive to the coast for holidays, or visiting local markets, but her family around the table were less impulsive after having waltzed through the corridor of time. For them, freedom meant a whole lot more.

Her uncle Khalid told her of a time when he was a young man who carted boxes in his beat-up van for extra cash. Financial pressures mounted when he and Amina's aunt Jameela found themselves expecting their first child. Whether sunshine or snow, Uncle Khalid got up at the crack of dawn every single day to deliver parcels all over the city before shuttling to the office where a day-job was waiting for him. Today, he was reaping the rewards of the seeds he had sewn back then, and hoped that Amina's education would yield her a good crop too.

Amina hugged her uncle. It was gratitude for the sacrifices they all had made to put her through university. She had always been very close to her uncle and aunt. She sometimes even thought of them as a second set of parents, if ever she needed.

Over dinner, they discussed where Amina could seek an internship to bring credibility to her pharmacy degree. That raised all sorts of further questions, like where she would live, or if she had paid enough attention to her chores to know how to feed herself and do the washing. They laughed, but Amina had suddenly become aware of all the things she now had to do because she had graduated in a career that she hadn't chosen for herself.

Everyone had talked her out of becoming a veterinarian when she applied to university because it just wasn't prestigious enough. A pharmaceutical education, however, could be used in the research of many diseases, and perhaps even help to change the world. That was the magnitude of potential Amina's family had seen in her, and they pretended to know better simply because they had lived longer than she had.

Their love for her was indeed real, though it did skew their perception of who she was as a person. Her own parents couldn't see her love for animals and, because she had allowed it, Amina's life was now cultivated by someone else's ambitions. It was tantamount to living a lie, and sitting amongst the people she loved most in the world, Amina began grasping the first true lessons of adulthood. It was difficult to swallow, but Amina saw clearly that it wasn't necessary to like those whom she loved.

The revelation turned a victorious night into the saddest dinner of Amina's life, and the brand-new car parked outside the restaurant seemed the perfect gift to just get the hell out of there.

When the memory faded, Amina found herself still struggling with the lawnmower. Every time she yanked the starter cord, the lawnmower coughed, but just wouldn't start. Still, Amina couldn't stop herself from trying, and kept yanking the starter cord over and over again in the hope that something in her life would miraculously start working.

That she struggled to perform such a simple task made her feel stupid indeed, and alienation became Amina. The bitter truth of feeling entirely alone could not be avoided, and that's when Amina stopped.

She let go of the cord and sat down on the lawnmower. Undermining herself was just a waste of time. From that moment on she was going to establish boundaries. She was also going to police them diligently, and make sure that she put herself first. It was painful to realize that Amina only had herself to rely on, and she calmly put her hands back on the lawnmower's handlebars. It suddenly jumped to life. The starter button was there all along. She just didn't have the eyes to see it before.

She was then forced to call upon her wits as the lawnmower leapt ahead like a rodeo horse. Struggling for control, Amina rode it right over Bruno's tail, and a tuft of hair was ripped from his body. It floated gently to the ground while Amina yelled at Bruno that he best believe she was invisible.

"Bruno-oooo!" Khadija yelled from the kitchen window.

She dropped what she was doing and waddled out of the kitchen on her short legs, stomping across the veranda, past the bannister, and over the lawn to rescue her dog. Khadija fell upon Bruno, and hugged the furry beast as if her own life depended on it.

"You're hurting me," he growled, but not everyone understood dogs very well.

They watched Amina zig-zag across the lawn, cursing the damned machine for having a life of its own. She managed to steer toward the gate, beyond which was her freedom, and her children.

Being a novice at gardening though, Amina drove the lawnmower over a patch of stones. The blades were spinning in full motion, and scattered a heap of stones in every direction. Bruno and Khadija ducked for cover while some of the shrapnel hit a nearby drum and played a tune. More stones thudded against Anwar's brand-new car, and at least one went crashing through the window.

Woo! Woo! Woo! The car alarm blared in the silent night.

Doof! Doof! Doof! Two men could be heard stomping down the wooden stairs in the farmhouse. Mevlana and Anwar rushed outside to see what the commotion was.

As much as Amina had struggled to get the lawnmower started, she was as clueless as to how to stop it. Eventually she jumped off and rolled on the ground as the lawnmower crashed into the shed, and killed its own engine. Amina got to her feet, and wiped the dirt off her face. Mevlana and Anwar were standing on the veranda, the former's teeth clenched, and the latter pulling his own hair out.

"My car! My car!"

Amina did the only thing she knew how to do when her independence became overbearing. She ran!

Besides, no one could catch her if she was invisible. Soon there was some distance between her and that dreaded farmhouse. The wind blew in her hair, and her escape became all the more exhilarating. The sheer force of her feet thrusting on the ground, throwing her one lunge ahead at a time, allowed the fresh country-side air to penetrate her, and clear the clouds in Amina's head. In her mind's eye, Amina had already jumped the gate and reached the road. She had already hitch-hiked to Pa's house and tore the door down to hug Mo and Fatima. That image exploded as surplus energy in her gut, and Amina's limbs carried her faster than any pharmacist had ever run before. She could feel freedom on her face. She knew where she was going, and that was no story that she had made up in her head. It was simply what she wanted to do.

Rather unexpectedly, she ran into the old farmhand with his one grape-eye. Undeterred, Amina swiftly changed direction, even though she heard his pack of dogs barking behind her. Amina refused to stop until she had escaped the farm, and this life that she didn't want anymore.

She was pretty sure that there was a word to describe such a vibrant state of being, but was still searching her mind for it when the thorn bushes on the perimeter of the farm shook like an earthquake hit them.

Amina had run right into them.

Her limp body was carried into the kitchen and laid on the table. Thorns still stuck in her limbs, and her clothes were ripped, soaked in blood. Lying there, she looked like a life-sized voodoo doll.

"Why are you doing this to yourself?" Anwar cried.

He caressed Amina's face the way he hadn't in ages as the thought of losing her finally struck him. Ever so carefully he pinched a thorn out of her face and, when her cheek bounced back, Amina coughed to life again.

For that one moment, while Amina was battered and bruised, and Anwar was doting generously over her, they were a couple again. They saw eye to eye and, amidst her own confusion, Amina recognized the tinge of green in Anwar's eyes that she had always found so enchanting. He loved her, and that was an indication that they could still make it.

Outside their little love bubble though the kitchen was in a frenzy. Mevlana shouted for the dog to be kicked outside, and Khadija banged the screen on the kitchen door shut. She then ransacked the kitchen for emergency supplies, and out of one cupboard tumbled a cereal box. It crashed on the floor and spilt its contents. Mevlana cussed at Khadija and, when Amina gleaned what the fuss was all about, she noticed that her handbag was sitting in the cupboard where the cereal box ought to have stood. She thought that she had forgotten in the lounge, but it was deliberately stolen.

Mevlana swatted Anwar out of the way to inspect Amina himself.

Khadija brought him a clean rag, which he dipped into a dish of warm water and squeezed over Amina's face. That was the way to wash an apple, and Anwar was flabbergasted. Amina's wounds needed far more attention, and Anwar hopped behind Mevlana's broad shoulders in an attempt to supervise the mystic. But Mevlana threw the rag down and began laughing.

Anwar and Khadija stood by wondering what was going on when Mevlana pried Amina's eyelids open and examined her pupils. He was satisfied by what he saw, and giggled.

"She fell apart," he smiled, "the diagnosis worked."

Chapter Five

Bang! Mevlana slammed his enormous hand on the kitchen table. Khadija kept her gaze low, but noticed that the collars of Anwar's checked-shirt still stood proudly and the crease in his khaki pants held firm down the length of his legs. He didn't seem like a man who liked being told to shut up.

"She needs care," Anwar argued. "I'm taking her to the hospital."

"If you think doctors can handle the consequences…" Mevlana replied, deadpan, from the other end of the table.

It occurred then to Anwar that he didn't even know what the consequences were, let alone if they were dire. That's when the itching in his crooked little finger warned him to listen first.

Mevlana took the cue. He reached for a box of chalk on the shelf behind him, and removed a stick. With it, he drew a circle on the kitchen table. A few strange symbols were then added to the circumference. Khadija dropped the grimoire he regularly referred to in his hand. The mystic slid his fingernail along the ream of antiquated pages and, at once, flipped the book open to the precise page he was looking for. On it was drawn a diagram that matched the one on the kitchen table exactly. Mevlana copied the spell alongside onto a notepad, tore the sheet off, and set it alight in his hand. His palm was carefully tipped over, and the fire fell into the circle.

Mevlana's face was imbued with a yellow glow. Anwar swore that the temperature in the kitchen had suddenly dropped when the mystic's eyes suddenly rolled over and glared a stark white. His teeth grinded against themselves as the most obtuse way to recite a spell, and the sound of clicks and hisses echoed in the farmhouse kitchen. It may have been a foreign language, but equally likely to be gibberish too. Anwar's brows knitted. He crossed his arms, partly to keep the cold at bay, but also because he had seen talented tricksters before.

He quickly changed his mind though when an eerie voice began booming in his head. It wasn't Anwar's own, but it was distinct enough to be understood.

"Something else it is. Inside her. Pulls strings. She gone mad," the voice said.

A tingle ran down Anwar's back, and it wasn't the result of magic at all. He was utterly shocked and, try as he might, couldn't shut the voice out of his head. Anwar's inner ear was forced to heed the warning that Amina was a victim of demonic possession.

The voice said that her choices were being influenced by a creature called a Jinn. It was fashioned out a smokeless fire, could travel vast distances in time, and had entered Amina through the nape. That was where the door to human consciousness was located. Anwar had always believed in seeing as a measure of truth but, when he felt behind his own neck, there was no handle or doorbell there. The strange voice, however, still echoed in his head and he realized that Mevlana was communicating with it. Anwar was somehow privy to that conversation.

"Slowly, slowly. Take woman away. Alone. It with her. She for it."

The creature possessing Amina had a purpose. It wanted to enter the human world, and found in Amina a physical vessel to inhabit.

"Why?" Anwar yelled, now engaged, but the spell had burnt out in the centre of the circle, and the connection was cut.

The kitchen warmed up again, and the light seemed to have also brightened. Mevlana's pupils swung around in his eyes as he snapped out of the trance.

"How would you like to be prisoner in your own body?" Mevlana asked, his big glaring eyes mesmerizing Anwar.

Just as his own mind was invaded moments ago, the idea of being conquered by some beast terrified him. He began to get an inkling of the suffering that Amina was experiencing during her episodes.

It turned out that the voice Anwar had heard in his head was an interdimensional creature who Mevlana employed from time to time as a consultant in the ethereal world that existed alongside theirs. But Amina didn't have the luxury of knowing what was going on.

"She's deliberately hurting herself," Mevlana explained, "which is why a hospital will only fix her body. But inside…soon the Jinn will find new tricks to draw her away from this farm, and your family, and from you."

"So, Amina trying to run away was its trick?" Anwar asked, somewhat confused.

Mevlana nodded. It was how he knew that the diagnosis had worked.

The episodes that Amina was experiencing were really bouts of fuzzy logic that Amina thought made for perfect sense, but was nonetheless irrational. By skewing her perception, and interfering with her choices, the jinn made Amina feel as if she was acting out of her own accord.

"So long as we try to rescue Amina, the jinn is in danger. It doesn't like that," he explained.

"How can we help her?" Anwar asked.

"Everything costs!"

Anwar bit his crooked pinkie finger, tempted to ask Mevlana if he accepted medical insurance cards. A hospital surely would. Just as he did in all his business dealings, Anwar was forced to calculate how much his wife's sanity was worth. It was no easy task either to think objectively about someone Anwar had shared a life with for so many years. In that time, Anwar had realized that Amina was different to anyone he had ever known, and that was precisely the difficulty in deciding whether to accept Mevlana's help or not.

When Anwar asked to see Amina, he was led up the old home's wooden staircase, and to a door outside which Bruno was standing guard. Khadija unbuckled a ring of keys from her waist and unlocked it. What Anwar saw within was a sorry sight indeed. Amina was lying on the bed, bloody and bruised.

Anwar immediately rushed to her side, only to find that a chasm between them had to be crossed first. As soon as she laid eyes on him, Amina pulled her hands and kicked her legs violently. She only managed to struggle like a caged animal though as her wrists and ankles were tied to the bedposts. Anwar couldn't believe that this was what had become of the woman he loved, and slowed his step in an effort to prioritize Amina's well-being.

Khadija closed the door behind him, but also left it slightly ajar, and gently pressed her back up against the wall. Putting a finger to her mouth, she signalled Bruno to stay put.

Inside the room, Anwar crept up to the bed and sat down alongside Amina. He caressed her face. Despite the maddening glare in her bloodshot eyes, he picked up a cloth from the pedestal and wiped the caked blood from her brow. Amina too relented and collapsed in exhaustion. Lying there, she stared blankly at the ceiling in that dimly-lit wooden box of a room. She didn't even look at him, and the rejection melted Anwar's insides.

"It'll all be over soon," he whispered, but Amina still didn't respond.

Instead, she rolled her head on the pillow to spit at him but, when her eyes met Anwar's, they took her to a place she hadn't been for a long, long, time…

A much younger version of both Anwar and Amina were seated at the dining table in her parent's home. They were out of earshot, but Ma, Pa, and Amina's parents were watching them keenly from the lounge. It was customary in arranged marriages for parents to chaperone their children's first formal meeting as it was believed to bring about better decisions for the future. And Anwar needed help too. He nervously mistook Amina's thumb for a samosa when she offered him a tray of savouries. Everyone chuckled, and Amina was asked if she would like to speak to Anwar privately. She did.

The real matter wasn't whether Anwar and Amina liked each other. Their parents knew that the young couple were sneaking out of the house in the wee hours of the morning. They would park their car wherever they found an interesting view and talked for hours. Sometimes they guessed at what was happening in the windows of tenement buildings and, from the water tower at the top of a hill, they stared at the sky and unravelled themselves to each other. It was fun but, in all seriousness, Anwar's parents were at her home that day to support Anwar in asking for Amina's hand in marriage.

"Here's a cracker!" Amina's parrot chirped while she and Anwar stared at each other across the dining table. They both burst out laughing, and it broke the tension of being watched with so much hope. Everyone does, after all, love a success story.

"Well, the choice is really yours," Anwar told Amina.

"What do you mean?" she asked, then avoided stating the obvious by saying, "you have to choose me too."

"I'm here aren't I?" Anwar replied. His muscles were bursting out of his shirt, but he knew that they had no power there.

"Look, if you want to marry me, you should know I'm not the person you think I am."

"Tell me who you are then?" Anwar asked.

"I don't even know myself," Amina replied, dropping her gaze at the admission. "What you know of me is only an impression."

"No one knows anyone really. We're all discovering ourselves," he said. "We'll just be doing it together."

"How can you even be so devoted to me when I'm telling you that I have my own problems?" she whispered but, when Anwar's eyes met hers, he saw that Amina was really yelling.

"Because I made a choice to love you, and that precedes all other choices," Anwar leaned in to tell her.

"What the hell are you talking about?"

"Devotion!" Anwar whispered, and when Amina's eyes met his, she saw that he was really yelling. "There is no other choice in devotion but to love," he explained in a far more tender tone, and didn't have to say anything more.

"It precedes every other choice…" Amina whispered. She then considered herself lucky to have Anwar.

Back when that memory defined her life, Anwar had a vision to create a joyful family for both of them, and Amina was surprised that the future she had imagined for herself was being put to words by him. She agreed to marry him then, and gave him another chance now in that dreaded farmhouse.

"We have a future," Anwar said, and then told Amina that Pa had offered him the family inheritance if he could prove himself worthy of it. It came with conditions of course, but becoming the head of their family was an extension of a dream they had begun their marriage with.

It was the desire to build something meaningful together.

Even Khadija sighed at the intimacy of that moment. She stood quietly outside the door, holding her laughter with a hand over her mouth. Anwar and Amina were such romantics that it was almost tragic for two adults to be so naive.

"We can create whatever we want," Anwar continued in the room, "we just have to get through this one night. Whatever we did, together or to each other, is the past."

It was true and, even while tied to the bed like an animal, Amina's gaze softened towards Anwar. No matter what their marriage had turned into, they had created it together. To rescue their love, they needed to mutually breathe new life into it. Their future depended on it, as did their children depend on them.

Through the crevice in the doorway, Khadija peeped into the room to spy on why the conversation had suddenly died. What she saw sparked her curiosity. Despite Amina's injuries, she had lifted her head to peck at Anwar's nose. He smiled, and nibbled hers in return. It was a sweet thing to share, and Khadija fell dreamily back against the wall.

Anwar kissed Amina's forehead. It was all going to be over soon, he repeated, before standing up to leave. He caressed her one more time, and the gentle embrace stretched into a long and heartfelt smile at his wife.

Amina beamed a grin back. It seemed as if they were sharing the same thought, but hers was really a gesture born out of confusion. The truth was that Amina couldn't believe her ears.

A pair of birds were sitting on the ledge outside the window and, perhaps it was a hangover from the herbs she had sniffed earlier, but Amina easily understood their chirping. They were betting on whether she would forgive Anwar or not.

"Who doesn't like happy endings?" the first bird chirped.

"She's tied to the bed for God's sake!" the other tweeted back.

And so, the moment was lost in translation. Anwar left with a spring in his step while Amina's mind fought with itself. Wake up! She convinced herself that the idea of being a polyglot was certainly attractive, but believing everything she heard was dangerous.

Khadija pretended to have arrived with a bucket of water just as Anwar swung the door open. It was sitting outside the door all along, as a bowl for Bruno to drink from while on guard. Oopsie! She navigated around Anwar to avoid a spillage that Khadija knew would have to be cleaned up by herself, but he hardly noticed her while intoxicated by love-brain. To Khadija, Anwar looked like he had just rescued a puppy.

"Wow! That's one way to destroy a man," Khadija quipped while straddling across the floor.

She dropped the bucket of water next to the bed and sat down alongside Amina. Bruno followed her into the room. He bit the cloth on the pedestal and carried it over to Khadija. It got rinsed a few times in her sturdy hands before Khadija wound it around her finger and began nursing Amina's wounds. Slowly, and methodically, Khadija worked across Amina's arm, tending to each incision with such care that Amina's skin crawled. Amina was, after all, still tied to the bed.

"That must hurt!" Khadija jibed while yanking a thorn out of Amina's shoulder.

Amina cringed, but sneered right back, "that must too!"

She was staring at Khadija's cheek. The bruise left behind by Mevlana's tight smack to the face clearly showed three of his fingers. For once, Khadija didn't care to comment. She rinsed the cloth quietly to continue cleaning Amina's wounds.

"Is it just you and your husband who live here?" Amina asked.

Khadija sniggered. "Mevlana is my father."

"You're very dutiful to him," Amina remarked, surprised.

"We stick together. It's necessary!"

"Was that really necessary?" Amina asked, glancing at the painful bruise again.

"He's just looking out for me," Khadija replied after a pause.

"Looking out for you?" Amina frowned.

Mevlana slapping his daughter was an odd way to protect her, but Khadija explained that there were all kinds of creatures lurking about the ranch, and Mevlana was simply reminding Khadija not to step out of line.

"Oh, you mean for the greater good?" Amina asked, rolling her eyes.

"I need him," Khadija mumbled. The words were accompanied by a vacant look on her face, and that made them stand out as a loaded statement.

Amina read into it, and surmised that Khadija's relationship with her father was toxic. In exchange for her protection, Khadija was Mevlana's slave, and that made her a kind of possession for him to use as he saw fit. If

Amina were to guess, it was probably why
Khadija had taken a shining to her. Amina's
cheekiness toward Anwar, and Mevlana, had
made an impression on Khadija in the
bathroom earlier, and it now made sense that
a younger woman like Khadija may be seeking
some freedom for herself.

What Khadija didn't know was that, all her
life, Amina's wilful personality begot criticism
from everyone. She was constantly advised to
avoid rubbing people up the wrong way as it
would eventually leave her isolated. Indeed,
Amina did sometimes feel like she was living
the life of a soldier of fortune. Those
experiences had taught her though that
surviving wasn't a life at all. A life worth living
was filled with joy and sharing. That was true
freedom.

"I'm sorry I nearly killed Bruno," Amina said. He was the only creature Khadija had to share her days with on that desolate farm.

Bruno nodded, as if to say he had told Amina so. She was indeed out of her mind when she drove over his tail with the lawnmower.

"Accidents happen," Khadija replied, in a brighter mood.

She was so moved by the apology that she told Amina of the many adventures she and Bruno had enjoyed in the vast field that surrounded the farm. They spent entire days in the stony crags that rose above the land while hunting for insects, flowers and herbs that Mevlana needed for his work.

Khadija so delighted herself by her own story that she leaned over to nuzzle Bruno on the nose. He licked hers in return, and Amina startled at the familiarity of that gesture.

Oh Hello!

Pecking at each other's noses was certainly not a unique habit, but it was Anwar's and Amina's. They had exchanged a nibble just a few moments before Khadija had arrived, and Amina suspected that Khadija had a darker side.

"Aww! Ain't that a sweet thing the two of you do?" Amina asked, watching Khadija's reaction closely.

"Everyone's doing it!" Khadija quipped, and then got squeamish when Bruno licked her face again.

She ran her sleeve down her cheek to wipe Bruno's saliva off and, when she opened her eyes, Khadija found Amina reading her like a book.

"You've got blood on your face," Amina sneered.

"It's not a disgrace," Khadija replied, continuing to clean Amina's wounds quietly.

There was indeed a smear of Amina's blood on Khadija's chin, but she didn't know it was there.

In such close proximity to each other, Amina understood that it wasn't freedom that Khadija sought. It was belonging, and emulating others was her way to feel it. Khadija was a chameleon, and Amina had best watch out for her. That was perhaps what Bruno had warned her about at the gates. Having just seen Khadija's true colours though, Amina pushed her luck.

"Does your father know you might slap him back one day?" Amina asked. It seemed reasonable to think that, if Khadija was besotted by Amina's insolence, she may mimic it in time.

Khadija ignored her. She didn't want to talk about her dirty little secret, so Amina clenched her fists and lifted them up slowly, until the rope tying them down pulled at her wrists. Khadija watched the display. Everyone knew that fists were likely the most prominent symbol of freedom in all of history.

"Do everything twice," Khadija mumbled, "that's what I say."

Instead of reaching for the cigarettes in her bra, Khadija stood up and dropped the bloody cloth into the bucket. She carried the pail over to the door but, when Bruno followed her, she stopped and patted him back down again. Khadija then left Bruno behind while exiting the room. The door was closed behind her, but no key turned within to lock it. All that was heard were Khadija's footsteps dwindling down the hall.

Bruno turned to Amina and licked his lips. For dogs, it was a gesture of appeasement, and Amina agreed. Maybe people didn't deserve to be hated all that much.

Minutes later, Bruno had gnawed through the rope around Amina's wrist. She stretched her arm high up above her, and the blood within began circulating freely again. Amina's mind began clearing, and the intimate nuzzle she had recently shared with Anwar filled her with hope. She rested her hand on the spot where Anwar had sat alongside her on the bed. A trace of something was left behind. It felt authentic, and Amina's heart crooned that it was trust.

Her head, however, recognized that Brad was Anwar's elder brother, and the rightful heir to their family fortune. It didn't make sense that Pa would suddenly dispense with tradition to offer Anwar the inheritance instead.

Hmm! The conflict between her head and heart left Amina wondering if Anwar was just telling her what she wanted to hear when repeating that everything was going to be ok?

"Hey Bruno!" Amina called out, "is Khadija trustworthy?"

"Whar rhao whee rhov eh!" Bruno replied while continuing to chew through the ropes around Amina's ankle.

"Tsk! ...I know that dogs are a man's best friend!" Amina sighed, "but how do you know you can actually trust her?"

"Wharr! Wrr rhim phrr rhee rhur!" he replied through a mouth full of rope.

"That makes sense," Amina observed.

As a domestic dog, Bruno relied on Khadija to bath, feed and shelter him. That Khadija accepted and serviced his vulnerabilities made

Bruno believe that she was indeed trustworthy.

"Hmm!" Amina wondered, "how do you know she's not deceiving you?"

"Whoar rhon!"

"You don't?" Amina asked.

"Whaach rhish rhees rhao whow whrr!"

"Yeah, I suppose we should all trust our own instincts," Amina remarked. It was food for thought, and raised the question as to whether Bruno was ever disappointed by Khadija.

"Wrr ɟhɪm rhop rhee rhur rhaar!" Bruno replied while cutting through the last bit of rope.

"Time!" Amina mumbled to herself. It made perfect sense.

Even though she had trusted her instincts to risk both heart and person in a life with

Anwar, it was really time that told her whether someone was trustworthy or not. That applied to Anwar as much as it did to herself.

"I swear you're just like a human in that body!" Amina exclaimed. "I do like animals more than people."

"Whow rhee rha whif rhee!"

"Sure, I'll throw you a frisbee som…" Amina said, but stopped abruptly. "Tricks!" she murmured to herself, wondering if she was a victim of one.

The last bit of rope snapped and fell to the ground. Amina was free, and she swung around on the bed to sit up. Her brow knitted while weighing up the differences between what her heart felt about Anwar and what her mind was saying about him.

"Hey Bruno," Amina whispered, "what do you do if Khadija forgets you outside?"

"I'll tell her to throw a dog a bone," he replied, coughing a few loose threads of rope out of his mouth.

"Wow, your expectations are low!" she said pensively.

"Well, do you trust him or not?" Bruno asked.

"Sure I do!" Amina replied, but that was just the staid reaction of a wife. The truth was that Amina didn't know what to make of the conflict between her head and heart.

So long as she refrained from explaining how a cricket ended up in the groom's mouth at Leila's engagement, no mediation between Anwar and Brad could be successful. Brad would always think of the incident as an act of malice, and Anwar's integrity would forever be in question if he couldn't get his own wife to spill the beans. The family may even conclude that Anwar was helping Amina hide the truth. For that reason, Anwar was beholden to Amina to realize his ambitions to leadership, so Amina couldn't tell whether Anwar meant that everything was going to be okay for her, or for him.

The only thing she knew for sure was that she was a woman trapped on a ranch by some evil people. The facts were more trustworthy than Anwar, Amina surmised, and it was unfortunately necessary to get some short-term insurance.

Amina fell back down on the bed as soon as she tried standing up. Perhaps it was uncertainty that weakened her knees, or it could've also been referral effects of the herbal concoction she had sniffed earlier. But Amina didn't allow any confusion to deter her. Instead she mustered up enough determination to never ever depend on anyone again for her own happiness. Amina steadied herself as she stood up again, and carefully stumbled across to the window where she threw one leg over the sill.

"That's the wrong way!" Bruno barked, "it leads to the hospital." He was waiting for Amina at the door that Khadija had deliberately left unlocked.

"I'll manage by myself, thank you very much!" Amina replied while hauling herself up onto the window's ledge.

She wasn't exactly being sensible, but Amina didn't want to run into any unexpected surprises on the other end of that closed door. There had been just too many of those in a single night.

At stake were the lives of two little souls who Amina hoped with all her might were not lost somewhere, shivering from the fear that they had been abandoned by their mother. Her own heart burst with the feeling of home. It beamed out of her chest into the wide-open skies. It carried her sentiment across the barren escapement that surrounded the farmhouse, past the thorn bushes and vicious dogs that guarded the perimeter. With all the force of a familial bond, it smashed through the bricks and mortar buildings in which her children lay probably asleep, and penetrated their dreams with the reassurance that they were still loved.

But the ledge she was standing on was at the mercy of the howling wind, and it blew Amina's hair into a crazy mess. She steadied herself to scan the frontier beyond the farmhouse. The window she was climbing out of stood an entire floor above the ground, and only the insane would've attempted such a dangerous route to escape. Her battered and bruised condition didn't put her at an advantage either, but somewhere out there were Mo and Fati waiting for her, so Amina did what all mothers in her position would.

She took a leap of faith.

"Wait!" Bruno yelled, running up to the window behind her. If, at first, he had thought Amina was crazy for thinking that she was invisible, he now was sure that lunacy was her permanent disposition.

Amina's feet slammed onto the corrugated iron roof covering the veranda. It stood at a slant that Amina hadn't initially detected, so she slipped and fell onto her back. Gravity then did its work. Amina skidded fast and dangerously towards the edge. Desperate to cling onto anything, her heart pumped furiously, and her survival instincts took over. The hyper-focus was far from comforting as Amina was fully aware of her legs falling off the edge of the roof. It was higher than she had imagined, and she was moments away from letting the menacingly hard ground below catch her.

In her panic, time slowed down. If Amina was incapacitated by the fall, she feared never seeing her children again. In an instant, she pulled herself together.

Clarity helped her hand to find the gutter, and she managed to grab a hold of it just in time. Amina hung off the edge of the roof by an arm, swinging from the house like a pendulum. She caught her breath, and laughed like she hadn't in years.

It felt wonderful to be herself.

With a little ingenuity, her feet found a lattice that was grown over with a crawling vine. The thick foliage was sturdy, and allowed her to climb down safely. When her feet touched solid ground again, Amina was a new woman. She quickly spun around to surprise the old grape-eyed farmhand who was always keeping watch, but he was nowhere in sight.

Amina then snuck around the farmhouse to the backyard. There, she crept up to the kitchen window. The coast was clear, and the screen door left unlocked. Amina swung it open and tiptoed into the kitchen where smears of her blood had stained the wooden table. She was laid down there earlier while wounded, and remembered seeing her handbag hidden in a cupboard.

The first cabinet she ransacked was stocked with Bruno's treats but, in the next, she found the cereal box that had spilt earlier. Behind it, was her handbag. Miraculously, Amina fished her mobile telephone out of it without having to dig around for an aeon. She noted that trick for use on ordinary days, but there was no time to waste, so Amina dialled the emergency services.

"I'm being held hostage, erm, by two men and a woman," she frantically whispered into the receiver.

"We're tracking your location," the operator said, "can you hold on?"

"Erm, Hekport! It's a farmhouse in Hekport!" Amina exclaimed. She remembered the sign they had passed on the dusty road to the farmhouse.

"Can you be more specific?"

"No!" Amina whispered, trying to contain her frustration, "that's all I know. It's farmhouse, very old, and the people here…"

Amina's words trailed off when a terrible wailing echoed through the creaky old farmhouse. It shook the walls and rattled the tiles on the roof. It was even creepier than the howling wind outside, and sounded like the abysmal cry of someone who was so helpless that they had given up on themselves.

"Khadija!" Amina cried, recognizing the voice.

She hoped that Khadija wasn't being slapped around by Mevlana again for leaving the door to Amina's room unlocked. Guilt overcame Amina. She had coaxed Khadija into aiding her escape and, while Amina appreciated the gesture enough to raise concern for Khadija, she didn't want to jeopardize her own flight.

Choices, choices!

The telephone that connected Amina to her only hope of rescue was in her hand, but her freedom would remain no more than an expectation if the events of that one unpredictable night hung over her head for a lifetime.

"Hello? Hello?" the operator's voice repeated on the other end of the telephone line, but Amina had already dropped the phone.

She followed the cry through the passage. It led her to the lounge, where she found that it was echoing from somewhere up the stairs. Amina found herself sneaking back toward the place she had just escaped from.

Outside a door at the end of the landing, stood Anwar looking rather perplexed. He watched Bruno scratch at the door. Neither dared to force themselves into the room despite the terrible begging coming from within.

Anwar caught Amina's hand before she turned the door knob. He pulled his car keys out of his pocket and jiggled it at her. The domestic squabble didn't concern them. They could leave quietly, he meant to say.

Amina smiled. She was relieved to have not distrusted Anwar outright, and agreed to leave with him as soon as she discovered what the matter with Khadija was. Amina needed to know because people often ridicule the things that they don't understand. Even Khadija didn't deserve that.

No sooner had Amina swung the door open though, did she wish that she hadn't pried into someone else's business. Inside the room, the most horrifying scene accosted her.

Khadija eyes were shut, and her body strewn across the bed. Mevlana was standing over her, pulling at her feet, as if trying to drag her away with a sadistic grin. Khadija wailed helplessly on, but she was at the mercy of the cruel mystic.

Nothing was what it seemed that night though, and what Amina found in that room was actually a sick joke.

On the bedside table was a bottle of oil that Mevlana used to grease his hands and then rub his fingers between Khadija's toes. He pulled at each digit and scratched the tips of her feet before pressing his thumbs into her arches. Khadija wasn't sobbing from despair at all, Amina realized. Though she sounded like a wounded animal, Khadija's moaning echoed how immensely she was enjoying the foot rub.

"I got bored waiting for you," Khadija said when opening her eyes.

"I read you all wrong," Amina gasped. It was a grave error in judgement she had made indeed.

"Tsk! Assumptions-assumptions!" Khadija replied, true to her motto of doing things twice.

"You're as mad as he is!" Amina exclaimed, and Mevlana chuckled. That was no insult.

"Just because we're different from the people you know doesn't make us mad," Khadija laughed.

Khadija seemed to know all about ordinary people like Amina. She knew that they lived in their own little worlds, avoiding anyone and anything that didn't fit the standards that they were familiar with. The lives of common people were nothing more than aged recipes for living that were passed down from one generation to the next, and dogmatically repeating traditions that had outlived their time was the undoing of many. Like Amina, efforts to rescue ordinary people from themselves was met with resistance, because the temptation to be right was far too overpowering.

"What makes you any better?" Amina asked.

"Nothing!" Khadija replied, deadpan.

Mevlana bellowed so loud with laughter that Khadija couldn't contain herself either. The joke really was on Amina. It was by her own hand that she had relinquished any chance of escaping the ranch, and led herself back into the clutches of her tormentors. Being human certainly seemed to have its caveats.

"This is insane!" Amina yelled.

"Is it really?" Mevlana asked, setting Khadija's foot down on a pillow.

He turned to Anwar, who didn't have an opinion to share. Anwar's little finger was itching again, and he chewed on it quietly.

Mevlana reached for a glass on the side-table and filled it with water from the pitcher alongside. He gurgled disgustingly to muster up the greenest glob of phlegm in his chest, which he spat into the glass of water. The spit hung from his lips for a moment before dropping into the glass, and Mevlana then offered it to Amina.

"You won't listen to anyone," he said politely, "so let's test your sanity."

Amina wasn't afraid of him. Oozing grit, she snatched the glass and gulped enough of the water to puff her cheeks up. She then spat the whole disgusting mess back into Mevlana's face.

"Oh, look!" Amina feigned surprise, "I'm perfectly fine."

The mystic didn't seem perturbed at all, even though she threw the glass against the wall and smashed it to pieces. He squeezed the damp out of his beard with a sardonic grin that helped Amina see what she was perceived as when behaving insolently herself. That too was unexpected, so she turned to Anwar and told him that he was right.

"Tonight, this ends," she said. It was time to take responsibility for their own marriage.

When she attempted to retrieve the car keys in Anwar's pocket though, Amina found that her arm had gone numb. Her limbs were stiff, and her face was stuck expressing the last expletive that she had hurled at Mevlana.

Amina was frozen, rigid as a corpse.

Mevlana stood before her, watching the terror fill Amina's eyes as she realized that the water was toxic. He showed her his middle finger, before tapping it lightly on her forehead. Amina tipped over, and fell backward like a domino. Anwar caught her just before she banged her head. He then laid her body gently down, flat on the floor.

"Was that really necessary?" he asked.

"You paid for it," Mevlana replied, fishing a set of car keys out of his own pocket and handing it to Anwar, who exchanged it for the keys in his pocket. "Told you, hope is the most effective way to ambush a demon," Mevlana said.

"What about Amina?" Anwar asked desperately. "Look at her!"

"Well her mouth doesn't move," Mevlana replied with intent to scathe, "now she's nothing more than a blunt instrument!"

Behind her dilated eyes, Amina was fully conscious, and watched Mevlana inspecting the pitcher of clear liquid. The potion certainly did look like water, and it had easily fooled her. It was ludicrous though that Anwar and Mevlana thought that they were helping her. Intent didn't translate to action. Instead, their concerns for Amina's apparent 'episodes' only reinforced her notions that people could never be trusted.

Too often, the words that are said are not always heard for what they meant. Misunderstandings were then slept over, and emerged the next morning as hideous philosophies which people convinced themselves was the absolute truth. Ideological monsters then rallied support from their kith and kin, who themselves nodded their heads in agreement because they too needed backing for the fictions that they carried in their heads. Petty confusions soon grew into gigantic balls of crap that trampled all and sundry. In this instance, it amounted to Anwar believing that Amina was possessed by a demon.

…And he was the one accusing Amina of making up stories in her head. People!

Stiff as a plank, Amina was carried down the stairs by Anwar hauling her at the shoulders and Mevlana at her feet. The ceiling of that old farmhouse was in no better shape than the walls and plumbing. It hung here and fell there, and it was the blinding flash from a cracked light fitting that took Amina to a space deep within that was beyond the violation of her body and the twisting of her mind. It was a place that Amina unquestioningly trusted, and it was there that she had buried a secret that she hadn't dared to tell anyone.

Keeping it had angered Anwar, who then poisoned Amina's own children against her. She was now a corpse, thanks to a charlatan that Anwar couldn't see was masquerading as a mystic. Her family hated her and her friends thought that she had lost her mind. All the rejection in the world didn't matter as much as keeping that one secret, for it was all Amina had to negotiate her reunion with her beloved children.

That was the only thing that mattered to Amina and, if the sun was to rise again after that night, it would be the time to seek out a divorce lawyer. In the meanwhile, she watched herself be laid down in the basement of the farmhouse like a cadaver in a coffin, waiting to be abandoned.

"Pinkie Promise," she thought, reminding herself why she was enduring this fate.

"Pinkie promise!"

"Pinkie promise…"

Chapter Six

By the time Ma arrived in the bedroom, Fatima was crying, and Mo full of excuses. Lying on the floor between them was the sleeve that Mo tore off Fatima's pyjama during the fight. The children were put to bed an hour ago but, once again, it became apparent to Ma that something was bothering them deeply. She couldn't help but think that it was related to Anwar and Amina's disappearance that night, and thought to scold the parents just as severely as she cautioned the children that a torn sleeve was the least of their worries if they didn't get back into bed.

"I want to go home!" Mo cried.

"It's the middle of the night," Ma told him, "go to sleep."

"I want to go home!" Mo yelled again, stepping away from her. Ma didn't know how to tell him that she too was worried as to why his parents were unreachable that night.

"Okay," Ma said, "I'm going to telephone your mother right now and ask her to come and fetch you." Ma then turned to leave, but stopped in the doorway. "If she asks why you want to go home, what should I tell your mother?" Ma asked.

"She's trying to make me break my pinkie promise!" Mo yelled, pointing at Fatima, who was about to share her opinion on the matter but decided not to on account of the stern look she got from Ma.

"What pinkie promise?" Ma asked.

Mo bit his lip until Ma convinced her grand-daughter to press her palms to her ears. Fatima scowled, but obeyed.

"What pinkie promise?" Ma asked again.

"I can't tell you!" Mo replied.

"Who said so?"

"Erm, mummy," was Mo's answer.

"Hmm, why did she say so?" Ma asked, sitting down on the bed to draw the boy closer to her.

"Because it will get me into a lot of trouble," was Mo's reply. Ma was no sleuth but those words were too tempting to ignore.

"We don't want that now do we?" she said, and the boy nodded emphatically. Mo showed his trust in his grandmother with a hug.

"Ok, I'm going to call her," Ma said, detaching herself from the child, "erm, what should I tell your mother you didn't say?"

When Mo was done whispering in Ma's ear, she reassured the boy that his mother would be glad to know that he kept secrets as securely as a vault. Mo jumped into bed, satisfied, and allowed Ma to tuck him in. There was unfortunately nothing she could do about the sleeve lying on the floor, but managed to get Fatima back into bed too without a fuss by promising to buy her a new set of pyjamas soon.

"You've both been good children!" Ma exclaimed before killing the lights.

Back in the lounge, Pa learnt why Amina had laughed so heartily at the groom choking on the cricket at Leila's engagement party. He heaved a breath of oxygen from a tank and returned the surgical mask to it. Pa was relieved that the entire incident was just a comedy of errors, and negotiating with the Ebrahim's to mend Leila's marriage had become a rather simple task. Even they likely had the capacity to forgive childish innocence.

The pinkie promise that Mo made to his mother was the key to the riddle of the entire engagement fiasco.

After Mo had found the cricket in a flowerbed, he showed it to his mother, who then gave him a piece of barfi from the sweetmeats tray to feed it. The child must've been too enthusiastic and probably smothered the poor insect. Mo undoubtedly choked too when he realized that he had killed the cricket and, afraid to own up to it, squeezed the insect's corpse into the soft block of barfi to conceal his mistake. He then returned the barfi to the sweetmeats tray as if nothing had happened, and the rest was history.

As a mother herself, Ma could easily understand why Amina had refused to say a word about the incident.

Brad went as far as imposing sanctions on Amina's children after the Ebrahim's questioned what kind of family they were marrying their son into. Anwar blamed Amina for embarrassing him, and jeopardizing his quest to seize the family inheritance.

Everyone else didn't know what to say, and Amina couldn't say anything lest the intense conflict surrounding Leila's engagement came crashing down on her little son.

Mo was at the centre of the entire debacle.

Everyone was wielding their pitchforks, looking for a witch to burn. If all that vitriol led to little Mo being tied to a stake, then the boy's innocence would've been lost forever. Amina saved that child's life by taking on the immense pressure that followed the engagement debacle.

While Pa nodded firmly in agreement, Ma decided that it was imperative to continue protecting Mo, just as Amina had intended, when talking the matter over with the

Ebrahim's. Amina may not have figured out a way to guarantee Mo's safety, and kept resiliently shut about it while dealing with the situation, but Ma and Pa could carry the cause with certainty.

"You haven't said a word?" Ma asked, feeling a little guilty for monologuing.

"I'm tired," Pa replied, "I think I'll go to bed."

"Are you feeling okay?" Ma asked, checking his temperature with a hand to his forehead.

"Nothing's the trouble," he replied, "for once, everything has worked out just fine."

"Yeah," Ma agreed, "Amina turned out to be quite sensible after all."

"Please tell her that when you find her and Anwar," Pa said, pushing himself to the edge of the couch.

It was uncanny, but that reply sounded just like the one Ma used to extract Mo's pinkie promise. She helped Pa to his feet while wondering if his silence was really a reluctance to respond to the news. They were like the sun and the moon, the two of them, best friends who understood each other.

"Any idea where we can find those two?" Ma asked. She was testing Pa, of course, and the quizzical look he turned to her with said that that he knew this game better than Mo.

"Oh you know, keep trying their telephones," Pa replied.

"Is there anything we don't know?" Ma pressed on, and Pa flopped back onto the couch to make himself comfortable.

When she teased it out of him, Ma learnt that Pa had caught Amina and Brad quarrelling behind the shed on the morning of the engagement.

"Well they hate each other so they can't be having an affair," Ma remarked, then asked, "what happened there?"

"Something much worse," Pa replied, "little Mo is caught in the middle of something far bigger."

Chapter Seven

Playing on the telly was an old film about a woman who was being walked home after a date. She held tightly onto a handsome man's arm as they navigated the snowy night back to her place. He walked her up the staircase, and to her door, where they fell into a tight embrace. The couple kissed passionately, and then the man turned to leave because women in classical movies rarely undressed. He was pulled back though by an endearing glance from his date, who then invited him in for a nightcap. She smiled when the man took her hand, and led him through the doorway to her apartment building. Upstairs, romantic music ensued as two glasses of wine were poured. The woman left to slip into something more comfortable and, when she slid the doors to her boudoir open a few minutes later, she found her handsome acquaintance waiting for her with a rope. He was actually a fiend.

"Oh my God!" she shrieked, "you're the serial killer!"

Dat-tut-taa! Things suddenly became dramatic.

Amina startled awake. Next to her in the bed, Anwar was crunching his way through a bag of potato chips. If the old adage of reaching a man's heart through his stomach were true, Amina would've stuffed the entire packet into his mouth.

"Urgh! Watch that in the lounge will you," Amina moaned as politely as she could.

"I'd rather be doing something else," Anwar mumbled through the mouthful of crisps, and then ran his finger down her back.

Amina pulled the covers over herself. "I told you already," she cried.

Leila's engagement was in a week's time, and it was rumoured that her in-laws, the Ebrahim's, were an incorrigible bunch. Amina hadn't met them yet, but kept pace with Ma nevertheless in the especial effort made for the event to go off perfectly. Preparations had been going for weeks already, and Amina was exhausted. That, however, wasn't why she was annoyed at Anwar.

"I have to take Mo for a check-up tomorrow," she said.

"After that, will you stop punishing me?"

"Oh!" Amina groaned, this was about that. "I don't want to talk about it," she said.

"We'll have to," replied Anwar, "I've been accused of domestic violence."

Filling the dreaded silence between them was a cry from the pretty woman on the telly. The serial killer had subdued her and stuffed a pair of stockings in her mouth. He still looked rather dashing in his dinner suit when politely enquiring as to where she kept the clothing iron. The woman's eyes bulged. The newspaper called him 'The Anonymous' because he burnt his victims' faces off before killing them. None of the bodies he left behind could be identified by the police.

"This is really your problem to fix," Amina said.

"It's our problem," Anwar corrected her, "aren't we a family?"

"No! You did this!" Amina retorted, "you beat Mo mercilessly, and now that child is traumatized."

"I'll apologize to Mo, I promise," Anwar said, crumbs hurtling out of his mouth. "But you didn't have to take Mo to Brad…of all people Amina!"

"Brad's a doctor!" Amina shouted, but quickly calmed herself down. "He's our family doctor, and Mo is comfortable with him."

"Can't you see what you're doing?" Anwar asked indignantly, "Brad's the one spreading the rumour of my domestic violence!"

The truth was that Amina hadn't given Anwar a second thought. Nor did she care about the bitter fight over the family inheritance that Anwar and his brother had gotten into the night he arrived home in a foul mood. Mo had unwittingly triggered his father's temper when continuing to watch television instead of having gone for a bath, but Anwar didn't have to childishly displace his frustrations on Mo. Perhaps it was poetic justice that Brad then latched onto Anwar's violent spate, and used it as leverage to discredit Anwar. The reputational damage jeopardized Anwar's position in their squabble over money, and Anwar was sour grapes about the consequences of his own actions. He was now accusing Amina of betraying him.

"Listen!" Amina snapped, "Mo is the priority here. He's caught in the centre of this fight between you and your brother, and still thinks that he did something wrong."

"Cut the crap Amina, I want my wife to support me!"

"I'm not the irrational and psychotic woman that you're making me out to be, "Amina explained as patiently as she could, "I'm defending my child, and the family you belong to…so I am supporting you!"

"No! You're pushing me away when I need you the most," Anwar shouted.

"You need to take responsibility for what you did to Mo!"

Aargh! A shrill scream interrupted Anwar's and Amina's midnight tryst. The woman on the television dropped the telephone when she found 'The Anonymous' breathing heavily behind her. She was cornered after having somehow managed to free herself and call for help. She hoped that the emergency services on the other end of the line had written down her address before the line went dead.

The serial killer snatched her before she could slip away and wrung her neck. As the woman faded in his grip, the killer reached for the hot iron and held it close to her face. Just before destroying her identity though, 'The Anonymous' asked the woman if she had any last words. It was a courtesy, as he had enjoyed their date, but very few people go to dinner with their eulogies prepared. The woman was dumbfounded to say the least.

Suddenly the din of police sirens grew louder in the street below. Tyres screeched outside the tenement building, and the hubbub was quickly followed by a thumping on the apartment's door. 'The Anonymous' startled. He looked to the window to contemplate an escape, but grimaced when realizing that they were a few floors up. His capture was imminent. He turned back to his terrified victim with the hot iron in his hand.

Dat-tut-taa! The dramatic music cut the scene.

"If ever there was a woman who needed to be rescued," Anwar sighed, trying to snuggle up to Amina.

"The cops have arrived!" Amina retorted, pushing him off her. "Now go to bed."

"I will when it's over," Anwar snapped back.

He wasn't getting laid that night, but he wasn't Amina's lap dog either. She sighed from her end of the bed. Amina wished that Anwar would just admit when he was wrong.

The cops on the telly crashed through the apartment door with their guns pointing and their badges flashing, but they were too late. The woman was not just a pretty face. She was sitting over 'The Anonymous' on the floor, holding the scorching iron an inch away from his face, just in case he decided to scare her again. Apparently, a kick to the groin was effective enough to disable serial killers, and the bitten remains of his ear that lay on the floor next to them was a warning to all men who were hard of hearing. The killer's blood streamed down his neck, ruining his dinner suit, and he was a gentleman no more.

Neither was Anwar when he pulled Amina toward him on the bed. She bluntly rejected him, so Anwar switched off the television and rolled over angrily.

"Love you," he screeched before closing his eyes.

Amina closed her eyes too. Thank God, she thought, as Anwar was becoming quite unbearable trying to trade his guilt for sex. She resolved not to sleep with him until he made up with Mo. It wasn't a punishment at all. It was a lesson her husband needed to learn.

The next morning Amina unsuspectingly walked into a barrage of Persian rugs, brass ornaments and doyleys. The trove of antique artefacts were gathered in Ma's garage. They had been delivered there to select decorations for the marquee that was to be pitched in the backyard for Leila's engagement. Amina was expecting to choose from colourful glass objects and rich fabrics to make young Leila's big day a fashionable one, and worthy of the society pages, but Ma may as well have brought the bride and groom in on horses judging by what she had in mind.

Worse still, Ma's archaic tastes were being endorsed by a child. Mo delighted in the variety of things to push, prod and pull, and snatched his hand away from his mother to explore the exotic treasures.

"Don't break anything!" Amina yelled, while beginning to count the hours in her head. After being deprived of sleep the previous night, this was going to be a long day for her.

"He's just a child," Ma remarked, pleased at the plethora of junk in her garage. Amina's diffidence was apparent, so Ma asked if Mo had become hyper-active since he was beaten by Anwar.

"I think so…" Amina replied. She was concerned that her son was imbibing the anxious atmosphere at home, but didn't want to discuss their domestic affairs with her mother-in-law.

Instead, Amina began inspecting the loot. When she came upon an archery set, it became necessary to query Ma as to what ambiance she was hoping to achieve for the engagement ceremony.

Ma had borrowed the idea of a Middle-Eastern theme from a popular television show that the Ebrahim's mentioned having watched religiously. Mrs Ebrahim, Ma said, was so captivated by the cultural history featured in the show that she even served cupcakes with marzipan swords on them the day that Ma and Pa visited them to set the date for Leila's engagement.

Because the Ebrahim's were notoriously difficult, Ma thought it a good idea to fit the event's décor to their traditional whims. She hoped that familiarity would make the Ebrahim's feel comfortable on the day. It was an astronomically large effort being made for people who Ma wasn't sure how to satisfy though. Amina didn't want to hurt Ma's feelings, but did wonder what harm there was in just being themselves?

Before she got her point across tactfully though, the helmet above a chainmail set crashed on the floor and rolled to her feet. Mo stood by, pretending that the armoured suit was alive, and lost its head of its own accord.

"Come here!" Amina yelled, and the boy instantly obeyed. "Ma and I are playing a game of 'circus'. We want you to play with us."

"How do we play that mummy?"

"It's just like musical chairs, but different," Amina explained. "I'll point at something, then you have to move it to a place where I point to next," Amina said, and that was how she and Ma began working through their décor choices.

With a stack of magazines, they sat upon garden chairs in the garage and instructed Mo about. Rolling out a rug kept him busy, and dragging a wooden chest into place tired him out enough to stay out of trouble while Amina and Ma sparred over the layout. Once they had completed arranging their first stage setting, Ma and Amina stepped back to evaluate it.

Ma was quick to the draw.

To her, it was perfect. The tall brass pots made the layout look like the Ebrahim's living room, but before she threw a few doyley's about to accurately capture the face of tradition, Amina threw a spanner in the works. She walked over to the centre of the setting and stuck a pose. Amina almost disappeared while camouflaged by the dizzying array of colour embedded in the traditional designs, and Ma got the point. Leila and her groom needed to stand out rather than blend into the background at their own engagement party.

Since mothers-in-laws are entitled to victory by default, Ma pointed out a picture in another magazine. It was dull, but had potential, so Amina made a few tweaks. Mo huffed and puffed as his tiny hands struggled to roll up one rug and replace it with another across the garage floor. He then dragged the wooden chests and brass ornaments clear of the setting while Amina replaced them with pot plants and vertical drapery as the backdrop. Two occasional chairs placed in the centre of the ensemble saw the design take shape. It was simpler and more elegant, Ma agreed.

Tradition didn't have to be staid, but the Ebrahim's unfortunately were, and when Amina returned from the kitchen with a few drinks, Ma had made a few tweaks of her own. The women then began arguing in much the same way that Mo would insist that crayoning outside the lines in his colouring book was okay. He lost interest at that point in the game of 'circus' anyway, and took his glass of juice to enjoy somewhere else.

"Why don't we try do this in our own style?" Amina asked, handing Ma a glass of juice to sip on.

"Will they like it?" Ma replied.

"Let's share what we're about too," Amina explained, "y'know?"

"I think this looks like the Ebrahim's dining room," Ma observed more confidently.

"You're probably right," Amina replied, employing some diplomacy, "all that brown and orange, erm…"

"Gives it colour?" Ma ventured.

"…Makes it look like a kitchen from the seventies!" Amina said.

They both burst out laughing, and frankness luckily prevailed. It was agreed that the criteria for a special occasion was that everyone in attendance enjoyed themselves, not only the Ebrahim's.

"Okay, I give up," Ma exclaimed. "I don't know what the Ebrahim's will approve of."

"We're not contortionists, so let's not get ourselves all tied up in knots."

"Yeah…" Ma pondered at their handiwork, "this looks like a circus."

"Let's be authentic to ourselves also then?" Amina asked, and Ma nodded. It was the best idea they had yet.

"Mo? Mo?" Amina yelled, but the child was nowhere in sight. It was time to go, and Ma agreed to seek out a professional decorator before they went in search of the boy.

"It's terrible that he's caught in the middle of Anwar and Brad's battle," Ma said.

"I'm stressed about it too," Amina replied. "Things have really gotten out of hand."

"Don't I know!" Ma cried. "I grew my sons up on the principle that they stand up and be men, and now they're stuck in those roles without any feelings."

"That's what I've been telling Anwar," Amina exclaimed, "he's Mo's father!"

"Maybe he just doesn't know how to take responsibility for what he did?" Ma wondered.

Amina understood a mother's bias, but nipped the matter in the bud.

"It's just like the décor," Amina remarked, "be yourself…Anwar is usually wonderful with the kids."

"Urgh, this child!" Amina grimaced when finding Mo in the garden, busy tearing the flower bed apart. She gave Ma her handbag to hold, and ran off. Pinching him by the ear, she dragged Mo back to Ma.

"Sorry!" Amina cried, "he seems to think that violence is okay ever since he was beaten up by his father."

Ma bent down to give Mo a kiss, though he didn't like it very much. The women hugged, and Amina pulled Mo along with her to the car. She just didn't know what to with him.

For all the preaching she had done that morning in favour of authenticity, Mo's newly acquired penchant for violence was a reflection of their situation at home, and Amina was a part of it. His behaviour mirrored who Amina was too. While authenticity was a wonderful thing, it also had a flip-side. Did anyone really want to see such glaring truths about themselves?

"What about the sweetmeats?" Ma shouted at Amina from the door.

"I'll take care of it!" Amina yelled back, and then drove away.

Cruising along the highways and byways that led to the city, Amina wondered what the hell she was doing by denying her husband sex. In all honesty, it was an act designed to hurt Anwar, just a smidgen, to force him to stand on his own. Once he realized the toll that the family feud he had picked to fight was taking on him, he would likely return to the sanctity of family for his own comfort. The children too would then have their usually sensitive father back. But as the traffic signs passed in and out of view, and she followed the ones that led to her destination, Amina wondered if she was merely telling herself a story to justify her behaviour. The bare fact was that she was using sex to exercise control over Anwar. Protecting her vulnerable son was felt as a motherly instinct within, but the ferocity with which she executed it also severed a connection with her husband in favour of one with her children.

Now, what kind of love was that?

What it wasn't was quickly clarified at Brad's medical suites. After parking the car and riding the elevator up to the reception, Amina discovered that Brad had postponed Mo's check-up appointment. Instead of having the boy's bruises seen to immediately, Amina was handed a clipboard with a form to fill in.

Apparently, she had skipped the formality of registering Mo as a patient at their clinic, and the nurse was asked to follow due process with Amina.

Given that Brad had known Mo since the child was born, it was quite an insult. Amina guessed that the administration was being suddenly thrust upon the child due to his father's dispute with his uncle, and Mo was once again caught in the middle of their fight. It was ridiculous to victimize the child, but people often are absurd.

Doctor Brad, tall and authoritative in his white coat, arrived to deliver an uncomfortable salutation. A few cold pleasantries were exchanged before Amina learnt that they could stop tip-toeing around each other soon.

A meeting was setup by Pa to deal with Anwar and Brad's dispute. It became necessary after Anwar challenged the tradition of the eldest son being the default beneficiary of the family's inheritance. Anwar believed that times had changed, and the family would be served better with a leadership that adapted to their needs. Of course, Brad scoffed at the idea.

Amina was glad that they were headed toward a truce, but her child was standing there waiting for medical care while 'Doctor Brad' was trying to convey the message that his brother still had the nerve to send the son he beat to the man he was insulting. It now made sense to Amina why Anwar had accused her of betraying him, but choosing sides was not her concern. Her son was.

Brad couldn't see that though. He didn't allow Amina to join Mo in the examination room. She argued that it would be helpful to observe the treatment to continue proper care at home, but Brad thrust the clipboard into Amina's hands and disappeared with Mo behind a door. Perhaps it was best that Amina avoided Brad too. She may have choked him as stringently as she was handling Anwar back in their marital bed.

Amina tossed the administration aside, and sat down to page through an ancient edition of a fashion magazine. The periodicals in Brad's waiting rooms were as dated as his ideas, and so Amina paged through the past to while away the time. In any case, her mind had never stopped cogitating since finding Mo tearing up Ma's flower bed, and it was when Amina fell upon the picture of a tiered white and pink birthday cake that her rumination finally flowered…

Surprise!

A teenaged Amina was shocked when walking into the door after a usual day at school. She didn't expect her parents to be home, but there they were standing with a pink and white cake that glowed cheerfully in the flames of the candles on top. Behind them were her uncle and aunt, and a huge pot of tea sat steaming on the dining table.

The five of them sat around it, and Amina peeked beneath to spy on where her cousins were hiding. She treated them as brothers and sisters, and no family occasion was complete without them. When Amina popped up in her chair again to ask after them, she realized that the rest of the family wasn't invited. The nervous faces staring back at Amina left her with a giddiness within that was desperate to decipher what exactly was going on.

To avoid the uncomfortable silence, Amina turned to the stack of presents alongside. The distraction proved futile though when Mum took Dad's hand while watching Amina. A tear welled up in Mum's eyes, and Amina then understood that they had something to say. She assumed it was bad news, but couldn't fathom why they needed a birthday cake to convey it. It was then that Amina learnt, sixteen years ago to the very day, she was her parent's gift.

In actuality, Amina's cousins were really her brothers and sisters, and the uncle and aunt whom she had always been very close to were her biological parents.

Amina was adopted by her Mum and Dad after an accident in which they couldn't fall pregnant. They really did want a family, but nothing medicine had to offer at the time was working for them. No one had known about it except the four of them sitting at the table, and they had decided to keep Amina's adoption a secret until that day, Amina's sixteenth birthday.

"It was both sad and happy at the same time for us," Aunty Jameela said.

"On one hand we were letting a child we loved dearly leave our home," Uncle Khalid explained.

"…But on the other hand," Amina's Mum said, "we were overjoyed to start a family." Dad squeezed Mum's hand as the tears streamed down her face.

"We agreed," Aunty Jameela continued with tears in her own eyes, "that you had to be a part of everyone's life so you didn't feel like you missed out on a wonderful childhood."

Amina stared at her real mother, unable to describe what it felt like to suddenly see her as someone else. Her uncle Khalid too looked different to Amina, but that was because Amina was also looking at her own parents differently.

"We all love you," Aunty Jameela said, "and want you to know that we're the same people you have always been able to rely on."

"You still can," Mum said.

A surprise for Amina indeed her sixteenth birthday was.

She understood why she had the same almond-shaped eyes and jet-black hair as her cousins, and why Amina felt so comfortable with them that she practically lived in their house when she wasn't at home. Somehow, their kinship was always known, but never articulated.

"Of course, you can call us whatever you like," her Uncle Khalid said, and Aunt Jameela nodded emphatically. They all looked at her expectantly, waiting for an answer, for it may have been a clue as to how Amina was feeling about the revelation.

"Erm," Amina thought out loud, "Uncle and Aunty Ditto?"

They all smiled, and the moment grew into laughter, and they enjoyed each other just as they had as a family thousands of times before. Amina told them that she didn't want any formal welcome from her true siblings as she was already a part of their family, and nothing needed to change. She then closed her eyes and blew the candles out on her birthday cake.

And as the air was pushed out of her, in the depths, Amina wished that the home around her wouldn't shake so violently. Questions were exploding in her mind, and the volume of them was overwhelming, but the throbbing in her belly was clear. It was the fear of not belonging anywhere, of being completely alone. The value of feeling connected was suddenly apparent to her, and Amina chided herself for having taken it for granted.

And when the flames on the candles went out, a wisp of smoke lingered.

Perhaps that was the very beginnings of Amina's episodes. At first, she felt just a little lost but, after a while, her mind ran at such a speed that Amina used to shut her ears just to try make it stop. Neither pills nor sleep helped. Even in the middle of the day she would suddenly find herself accosted by a panic that cut her at the knees and put her at the mercy of anyone nearby. To cope, she became obsessive, and clung to anything with the feintest promise of filling the void within her. Amongst those things, stories were the most effective medicine.

Like smoke, stories could take any shape that Amina wanted. They represented possibilities, and that was precisely what she needed to distract herself from the emotional tornado ravaging her within. An imaginative story could captivate Amina's attention, and transport her to a reality in which nothing affected her much. In stories, what she felt was of her own choosing, and when the characters in her world sounded and behaved like people that Amina could understand, she felt reconnected. It was why she amended reality into the stories she kept telling herself in her head.

To others, she appeared erratic, and was often advised to curtail her flights of fancy, but they didn't understand how rare love really was.

They just didn't know.

After blowing out the candles on her sixteenth birthday cake, and after that wisp of smoke had dissolved into thin air, Amina was never the same again. What happened that day was what she wanted to protect her little son from. She never wanted Mo to ever feel like he was being pushed around by the world, or worse, discarded like used tissue paper.

So, when Brad delivered Mo back to Amina in the waiting area, and said that he would send the invoice for treatment to Anwar, Amina readily agreed. For some people, money was more important than trust, and for them, kindness was limited to no more than a transaction.

When Amina gathered her things, and took Mo's hand to leave, the child looked up and smiled innocently at her. He was waiting for her, excited to hear what next they were going to do that day. For him, life was still an adventure, and she wished that she could wind the clock back to a time when she didn't feel so overwhelmed.

A few nights later, after Fati and Mo were tucked safely into bed, Amina found herself on top of Anwar in the throes of passion. Her hips were swinging like a flag in the free wind. Her moratorium on sex was revoked when Mo ran into the front door with an ice cream in one hand and pulling his father with the other.

Amina was worried sick after getting a call from the school that afternoon. Mo had gotten into a fight on the playground, no doubt because the example of violence that was being set at home had escalated. The school was not impressed by his behaviour but, when Amina arrived at the principal's office to fetch her son, she discovered that Mo had already been picked up by his father.

Anwar turned the incident into an opportunity to teach Mo a lesson. He had become aware of the effect of his own behaviour on Mo, and came to his senses about what he had done to his son. Mo was taken over to the house of the boy whom Mo had bullied, and was made to apologize, but Anwar then took his son to the park where he too apologized to Mo. He admitted to the child that he had beaten Mo up unnecessarily, and that kind of behaviour was inexcusable.

By the time they arrived back home, Anwar had set a new example for the boy, and their relationship had been rekindled. The act had also restored Amina's trust in Anwar. When she heard that Anwar had skipped out on the important family meeting with Brad and Pa in favour of tending to his son's needs, Amina also discovered what was truly important to Anwar.

Her husband became Amina's hero once again.

When the television wasn't switched on, the gentle moonlight streamed in through the window with ease. It flooded their marital bed, and Amina watched her husband's face groaning with pleasure as she straddled him. Usually her eyes would be closed but, that night, she drank in the vision of him. Every twitch of his mouth, every moan, every gasp she watched with delight. Anwar was the object of her affection, and Amina didn't have to choose between him and her beloved son anymore. It wasn't just a relief. It was a dream fulfilled and, in that moment, she would've done anything for Anwar.

Splash!

The bucket of water thrown over Amina killed the last of the illusions she harboured. She was still paralyzed, courtesy of the potion she had mistakenly drunk. She could however feel every push, pull and pinch as she was flipped-up and tied to an icy cold pole in the basement of the farmhouse. If that bucket of water had done anything, it woke her up to her husband betraying her to his true agenda. Amina had never even conceived it possible to become a casualty of trust.

"Is this necessary?" Anwar cried.

Mevlana had mixed some dirt into mud with a stick, which he then used to graffiti a set of symbols onto Amina's forehead, hands and feet. A screwy vibe had overcome him, and his eyes were teeming with mania.

"We have to prepare her," Mevlana shouted.

"For what?" Anwar asked, prompting Khadija to giggle. Anwar was biting his crooked little finger, and even she had learnt that it meant he was feeling anxious.

She poured a glass of water from a pitcher and offered it to Anwar. "No!" he yelled. She shrugged her shoulders and took a sip herself. Perhaps he didn't trust her after seeing the consequences of Amina having misplaced her wits.

"The jinn that is possessing her won't go easily," Mevlana explained, "we have to weaken it."

"No, no!", Anwar replied, "You said that its tribe will come to exorcise and arrest it. That would stop Amina's episodes. That's what I paid for."

"That's not why you paid," Mevlana laughed.

He stopped painting the symbol on Amina's foot and stood up to face Anwar. "You paid to make your wife conform to your wishes, so she could stand beside you the way you needed," Mevlana said, then paused a moment to think. "I think you called it, erm, support?" he asked.

"What?" Anwar yelled, but his vitriol was clearly an overreaction. Those were his true intentions. Khadija laughed at him so hard that she needed another sip of water.

"You want your inheritance and, to get it, you needed your wife to do as you say," Mevlana explained, "…it's so obvious!"

"You can't read minds," Anwar sneered.

"I don't need to," Mevlana said, flicking the brown goo from the stick onto Anwar, "a man who so desperately needs to be validated stinks as much as this mud."

Behind them, Amina's gaze remained fixed ahead, but she could hear Anwar dusting the mud off his clothing. He didn't like being dirty. She was sure too that Anwar hadn't intended this to happen to her, but here they were anyway. There was no going back now and, without the benefit of mobility, all she could rely on was patience.

Anwar, on the other hand, seethed to mask his guilt. It made him sick to the stomach, so Khadija took another sip of water on his behalf.

"Take it!" Khadija offered Anwar the glass of water again.

He pounced upon Mevlana instead. With his limbs wrapped around the mystic's back, Anwar pulled at Mevlana's beard. The old man screamed, and spun around like a rodeo horse to thwart Anwar. Of course, being a much younger man with many hours of exercise beneath his belt, it was easy for Anwar to hang on to Mevlana's neck. Eventually he managed to choke the mystic, steadily bringing Mevlana to his knees. Khadija stood by laughing, and sipped her glass of water like it was a delicious cocktail at a cabaret.

"You misled me," Anwar shouted.

"You only see what you want to see!"
Mevlana wheezed while held in a pretzel grip.

Indeed, Anwar wasn't seeing clearly. His eyes were red from pure and unadulterated rage. He locked the mystic's throat in the crook of his shoulder and squeezed as hard as he could. Moments later, Mevlana was gasping for breath. The old mystic was pushed to the floor, where his violent passing was soon to be recorded, like a police crime scene, as the white-taped outline of a figure trying to run away.

The scant life left in Mevlana was used to raise a hand and beg Khadija for help. She gulped down the rest of the water, and Anwar instantly vomited.

Mevlana pushed Anwar off him. While he coughed to catch his breath, Anwar stumbled back and grabbed hold of an iron railing to steady himself. The retching didn't cease, and

Anwar lost consciousness. While Mevlana bootstrapped himself to his feet again, Anwar fell, banging his head on the cold iron before passing out.

How convenient, Amina thought. When Anwar was schooling his little boy about violence being morally wrong, he was full of courage, but facing his own actions was unbearable. It was the old 'do as I say and not what I do' shtick. She had placed her trust in Anwar, and put him on a pedestal all their married life. It came naturally too, along with love. But sooner or later it wore off, and then the faces of lovers that once appeared angelic turn devilish. It was now that Amina truly saw who she had chosen to be the father of her children, and she continued staring at the brick wall ahead of her, wondering if she was tough enough for love.

"Get him out of here," Mevlana yelled after regaining his composure.

Khadija slammed the glass down. After Anwar was dragged up the stairs, and the heavy door of the basement shut again, Amina was left alone with the vilest man she had ever encountered. It is said that patience is a virtue, but that was just what was colloquially said.

What happened thereafter in that cold and dark basement was best left right there in that hole beneath the farmhouse. Suffice to say that there was no demon possessing Amina, nor was there any jinn tribe that was coming to subdue it. Hell, who even knew if those creatures existed?

By Mevlana's own admission, Amina's 'episodes' were nothing more than the stubborn streak so typical of wilful women. The more Amina asserted her sanity, the more entangled she became in his elaborate ruse. He laughed wickedly for Amina was really the victim of her own pride. It blinded her.

And now Amina was the perfect tool to extract a fortune. Mevlana urged her to make herself comfortable, for she was going to be held in that basement until the entire stash was milked dry. In Anwar's desperation, he had revealed the details of his family inheritance. It was so large that it raised Mevlana's brow, and the mystic keenly planned to seize it for himself.

Preparations began soon after Amina's faux pas at the engagement. Anwar was asked to add a few drops of potion to her meals, which were designed to make her more pliable for the purpose. Considering the pressure that she was under, it happened much sooner than expected. Of course, Anwar thought he was helping his wife deal with an internal crisis, and meant well, but good intentions often blinded as effectively as pride.

Whatever Amina's fate was, she now understood that trust often implied an assurance that others behave according to her expectations. But that illusion was thoroughly trashed in that dark and cold basement, and it was in humility that she wondered why the 'emergency services' were called that when they were never around in an emergency?

Chapter Eight

The wind pushed the swing on the veranda. It creaked violently. The iron roof above clung for dear life onto the rafters of the farmhouse. It danced eerily. A tap dripped relentlessly into the ground. Its sobbing dissolved quietly. And further afield from that isolated farmhouse in Hekport, the tall reeds shuffled in the dark night, and the distant cries of creatures huddling in the stony crags bawled for mercy. The fog was being pushed from side to side across the outer limits and, from within that volatile night, a rumble began. Louder it grew, and deafening was the trembling of that lonely farmhouse clawing itself desperately to the ground. There was nowhere to run, or hide, when a black smog punched a hole though the haze and gained the definition of a creature with raging violet eyes and a fiery torso.

Whaaorr! It screeched, and slammed right into the old farmhouse.

Anwar fell to the ground and rolled on the floor. Instinct had him grab the lamp on the table, and he leapt to his feet wielding the domestic artefact like a weapon. Light does dispel darkness, and even the fringes on the lampshade trembled in anticipation of their duty, but there was no monster to strike. There was nothing to defend himself against save his own stupidity. All else was quiet.

Anwar had simply rolled off the couch he was asleep on in the lounge, and the roaring monster was nothing but the wind howling outside. His nightmare was vivid enough though to wonder as to the consequences of paying Mevlana to employ such creatures in aid of Amina's rescue. It was a sober thought, one that scared Anwar, and he made it disappear by wiping the sleep from his eyes.

The truth was that Anwar hadn't a clue as to how he ended up on the couch in the first place, and guessed that he might've blacked-out somehow.

The air was crisp with the coming morning when Anwar opened the window. The farmstead was otherwise deserted. No dogs were lurking about, though Anwar was weary of their master with the one grape-eye who was always keeping a watch. He was distracted though by the lonely cigarette butt that the wind had pushed up against the bannister on the veranda. It reminded Anwar that Amina had been there recently.

Anwar checked his wristwatch. Soon the dawn would break, and he would have to face his children. He couldn't do that without their mother.

Anwar trailed through the ghastly farmhouse in the dark, to the kitchen where he poured himself a glass of water from the tap and gulped it down. Behind him, on the counter, was a murky silhouette of a shape that he recognized. It was Amina's handbag, and alongside it was her mobile telephone and a box of cereal. He craved breakfast but ignored his grumbling tummy in favour of checking Amina's phone. It was dead, but down the passage was the door to the basement in which he had last seen Amina.

When Anwar snuck up to it, and put his ear to the cold metal surface, the door kept its secret. It was locked, and Anwar could hear nothing through it. Then his eyes shot up. There was a distinct shuffling upon the floorboards above.

Carefully, he ascended the staircase that led there. Anwar stopped on the landing to zoom into the source of the activity, but it wasn't clear anymore, so he proceeded to explore by himself.

There were three doors down the length of the passage.

The first opened up into an empty room, so Anwar passed it by as he had no cause to hide. The next was the room in which Amina was held captive. The rag he had used to wipe Amina's brow still sat on the pedestal, but Anwar preferred to not dwell on the image of his wife in chains. It was then that Anwar startled. He crept up to the door at the end of the passage.

It was the same room in which Amina took the swig of water that turned her into a stooge, and Anwar approached with caution. The light creeping out from beneath the door suddenly stirred, so Anwar bent over to peep through the keyhole.

Inside, the occasional chair and table were still in place, as was the armoire that stood against the wall. Its door was swung open, blocking Anwar's view, but then a hand gripped the edge and shut it. Khadija stood there, counting a wad of notes that were bound by Anwar's own money clip. It was the cash he had paid Mevlana to rescue Amina. Khadija tucked it into her bra, and then moved to the other side of the room where the view through the keyhole was constricted.

Something was definitely fishy, Anwar thought, continuing to peep into the empty space.

The door then suddenly swung open, and Khadija stood there with Bruno, wagging his tail behind her. She wasn't the slightest bit surprised that Anwar was spying on her.

"Just in time!" she exclaimed. "Don't worry, everyone makes mistakes."

As she led him back to the basement, Khadija lectured Anwar on the virtues of doing things twice. An error only remained one until rectified.

Downstairs, Khadija opened the heavy basement door with a key that hung off her waist. Bruno was left outside to keep watch while Khadija pushed Anwar through the entrance and shut the door behind them. As Anwar descended another staircase, he was led into the belly of the farmhouse, where trepidation became him.

He first caught sight of Mevlana, who was crouched on the floor, licking his palms. The mystic's white cassock was frazzled at the seams, as if he had burst out of it at some point, but Mevlana paid no attention to Anwar. He was focussed on something else, and Anwar followed the mystic's gaze to find the product of his own good intentions.

Amina's feet were caked in blood, and lay asunder. Her bare legs ended at her twisted torso, which left her arms thrown to each side. Anwar couldn't even see Amina's face. Her hair was matted all over it but, there she was, naked and dead on the cold stone ground. Never mind her condition, the sight of her alone was utterly disgraceful.

Anwar rushed over to Amina. He fell to his knees and threw his coat over her. Cradling her in his lap, he gently swept the bloodied hair away from Amina's face. There was no way to undo the terrible error in judgement he had made while swayed by the magical thinking of superstition. He shook Amina's lifeless body desperately, pleading on behalf of their children for her to wake up, but good intentions don't always amount to great actions.

"What did you do?" he yelled. There was no reply from the mystic.

The shouting, however, stirred some life into Amina, and she gasped. She was alive! Anwar was determined to take her to the hospital this time, no matter what anyone said. He only needed Amina to hang on just a little longer.

Mevlana hopped off his haunches to reach for a crowbar that lay nearby, but Khadija patted him back down again.

"Wait," she said, allowing Anwar's rescue to unfold as it may.

"Everything's going to be okay," Anwar whispered to Amina.

This time he meant it, and the sincerity in his voice pried her eyes open. It raised a second wind within Amina, and she trembled as the energy coursed through her body again. When her limbs twitched back to life, Anwar found that Amina was no longer frozen by the vile potion she had drunk earlier. Amina was mobile and, in that bleak basement, Anwar resurrected the hope of seeing her children again.

Struggling to lift her arm, Amina managed to put her bloodied hand on Anwar's face. She caressed him, pulling him close enough to peck at his nose. The gesture overwhelmed Anwar, and he resolved to never fail her again. With gratitude, Anwar nibbled Amina's nose in return. It was their thing, a personable way in which they shared their affection for each other.

Anwar savoured the moment, and closed his eyes. A new dawn was rising. When he opened them though, he found the sentiment ruined and Amina staring back at him with a diabolical countenance. She was laughing at him.

Before Anwar could decipher what had possessed her to be so cruel, Amina sprung around like an animal and pulled Anwar's feet out from beneath him.

He banged his head on the stone floor. Vertigo robbed Anwar of his wits, and he was oblivious as to what Amina meant when told that it wasn't compulsory to like the people they loved. The words rang in his mind like an alarm bell, but Anwar couldn't respond as his eyes closed by themselves.

He was rudely awakened by a thump on his chest. A thick notepad had landed upon it. Anwar was comatose for who knows how long, and found Amina now standing over him with eyes that were narrow with vengeance.

"Write!" she barked, but Anwar failed to find any words. "A pledge!" Amina explained when Anwar inspected the notepad.

"A pledge?"

"Yes, write a pledge to donate your entire inheritance," she grimaced, chucking a pen at him.

"To whom?" he asked, still bewildered.

"To him!" Amina cried, pointing to Mevlana. It appeared that Amina had lost her mind, but she had come to understand that the promise of being rich was driving Anwar mad.

"What are you doing?" Anwar whimpered, "you're throwing away Mo and Fati's lives…our future!"

"You won't have any children by the time I testify in court that you paid to have their mother abused," she replied. Amina then sauntered over to fetch a crowbar that lay nearby.

"I was told that you were possessed," Anwar cried when she returned. "You have to believe that I acted on your behalf, for your own good…trust me!"

"Of course, I do," Amina jeered, "a woman should trust her husband always, shouldn't she?" She reminded Anwar that, if he insisted that she was mad, then she accepted the decree whole-heartedly. Anwar did, after all, bring her to the farm to make a dutiful wife of her.

"Write!" Amina screeched, but Anwar refused, and tossed the notebook aside. Amina watched it tumble away.

"Well that's unfair!" she quipped.

As a stalwart of their culture, Anwar had always encouraged Amina to put herself in the service of others, but he wasn't as charitable himself. Altruisms such as 'doing unto other as she would have done unto herself' were really crippling superstitions, and Amina was tired of playing second fiddle.

She let her knees give way and fell upon Anwar. Amina sat on him with all her weight pegging him to the ground, and then she pulled his hand toward her. When she flatted his palm, Anwar's crooked pinkie finger stood up on end. It amused her, so Amina pushed it down, but it jumped right back up again. The disfigurement had always made Anwar self-conscious, though it was time for Anwar to stop thinking too much of other's opinions. It was only the esteem of others that fuelled his greedy for money. To teach him a lesson, Amina swung the crowbar and slammed Anwar's crooked finger straight.

"My hand!" he yelled, his eyes bulging out of their sockets.

"You won't need it," Amina retorted, "your writing hand will do."

When Amina raised the crowbar over her head, Anwar finally realized that his wife was perhaps not as complicated as he had thought. Amina could be trusted on face value too. He sat up and reached for the notepad upon which he reluctantly scribbled the date. A swollen hand made the task rather difficult, but Anwar managed to scrawl the pledge anyway. She wasn't satisfied until he finally signed his life away.

"I don't know what you aim to prove with this," Anwar snivelled, ripping the sheet off the pad and tossing it to Amina.

"What do you mean?" Amina asked, "is this not how we respect each other?"

"You attacked me!" Anwar cried.

"As you betrayed me!" Amina exclaimed.

It was clear that, as man and woman, their relationship was now equitable.

"This isn't right!" Anwar shouted.

"Anything else is a double-standard!" Amina casually remarked.

And watching eagerly from the other end of the basement was Khadija. Before her was a spectacle of ordinary life that few could admit to. People could only be trusted to make their own choices, and this was the moment in which Amina was to make hers.

"Do it!" Khadija whispered from afar. This was what she was waiting for. "Do it!" she said again, clenching her teeth. All it took was a single strike.

But love affairs never truly end. They only change.

While Amina trembled with vengeance for being slighted by Anwar, a tear welled up in the corner of his eye and rolled down his cheek. Anwar looked like one of those traditional wailers who howled at funerals to amplify the sadness, and the visual transported Amina to a day when she had felt uncannily the same…

There was no way to avoid sorrow when she walked into the room where her Uncle Ditto flirted with death. His gaze kept falling vacant while his family competed for attention by gently pressing his hand and offering sips of water. Compared to their gloom, a journey into the afterlife with a black ghost seemed to be just the adventure that a man overcome with frailty needed. The promise of never coming back was perhaps even the climax of

Uncle Ditto's life, as what could ever be appreciated in life without a keen and constant remembrance of one's own mortality? There was only so much fussing anyone could make before extending their gaze over the horizon, and what another saw there was for their eyes only.

Amina had spent an aeon outside the door before entering that room. She slowly removed her shoes and placed them neatly beside the other pairs along the wall. She wondered if death was amused by people who thought that tiptoeing would keep it at bay, but the truth was that she fancied the thought as a way to avoid her own despair. A little tickle was helpful to assuage the guilt of having neglected to visit her biological father till his very last moments. Amina just couldn't bring herself to do it.

She was still struggling to open that door between herself and her father when death knocked from within the room.

"Who's there?" Amina asked.

"Malikal Mawt," boomed a hoarse voice.

"Malikal Mawt who?" she asked, but silence was the only reply, and Amina got the point. The time was now or never.

When she laid eyes on her father, Amina was flooded by emotions. His cheeks were sallow and he was reduced to the shape of a stick. The bedsheets weren't even dented by his lying there. It was as if he had already vanished, and that reflected how impersonal the silly name she called her biological father was.

She was a daughter who addressed her father as 'Ditto', as if a child could be fathered by more than one man. It may have been cute, but the moniker was also downright disrespectful.

Calling her father 'Uncle Ditto' was really a coping mechanism, a means to create distance that masked the abandonment Amina felt when learning on her sixteenth birthday that she was given up for adoption. What a waste of time and energy that had been. On his deathbed, where she faced true abandonment, Amina realized that it was her choice to keep love at bay.

Death grumbled, but allowed her father to cast Amina a single glance. She instantly felt the love that had always been there. Aunty Jameela, Amina's real mother, made a space for Amina at his bedside. It was taken despite the silent disapproval cast upon Amina by her siblings for having stayed absent until her father's very end. Death sat on the pedestal and laughed. He knew that Amina was gripped with the same malady that her father was. They both had to walk their paths alone.

As fellow travellers, a proper conversation between them was waiting for decades, but it still hadn't found the right time. Amina knew then that it never would. It didn't matter either as what needed to be exchanged between them couldn't be expressed. Words were merely a formality. True love could only be transmitted, and it was articulated in the steady gaze between Amina and her father. He was the one man that she never guessed to have had the power to make her feel like she wasn't alone in this big and wide world.

Death took offence at the intimacy and rose from the bedside pedestal to swing its sceptre at Amina's father. How dare the old man make another attempt at life on its watch. The blade struck fiercely, but couldn't penetrate the protective bubble that the bond of

parenthood had cast around Amina and her
father.

She then understood that her father had never
abandoned her. He couldn't. In his final
moments, the wisdom that no human being
belonged to another flowered in Amina's
heart. Each person was a life unto their own
and, even as a helpless new-born, Amina had
transformed both sets of her parents forever.

"There is…" her father managed to murmur
after heaving a breath, "nothing to prove."

"Dad!" Amina whispered back. It was the first
time she had ever called her father that.

The full meaning of that memory only
dawned upon Amina in the moment that she
wielded a crowbar over her husband's head.
Her children would suffer most if she struck
their father and, since they were Amina's
strongest bonds, Amina would effectively be
destroying herself by her own hand. She

dropped the crowbar. Though she had every reason to destroy Anwar, doing so was a fool's errand, and a poisonous seed wasn't planted that day.

"If you only knew!" Amina said, and stumbled away.

"Wait!" Anwar called out.

There was no doubt in his mind that she was referring to what had happened at the engagement, and perhaps was ready to finally say something about it. Anwar was now acutely aware that he had read the incident all wrong, but Amina was gone.

Amina dragged herself across the floor, and pushed past Khadija. She pulled herself along the railing, and up the stairs where she kicked the heavy door open and exited the basement. She had no intention of carrying the events that had transpired that night on the ranch out into the world with her. It simply wasn't worth its weight.

But something else was, and Khadija saw it in Amina.

"A pure soul!" she gasped. It was an unexpected surprise to stumble upon one, and that changed everything. Mevlana held Khadija's hand. He knew it too.

Khadija then followed the trail of blood on the floor, cursing all the while that she would have to mop the mess up herself.

She found Amina collapsed on the veranda, which was glowing in an alternating red and blue hue. Leaning over the bannister, Khadija spied a police car parked out front, and a pair of torch beams poking about the front of the farmhouse.

"You lost this," Khadija said, dropping the crowbar in her hand. It banged on the wooden floor.

Bruno licked Amina's cheek, but she wouldn't respond. "Maybe you're being too hard on her?" Bruno asked.

"She's proven herself," Khadija replied.

"Yeah, but don't spoil her," Bruno remarked, "hope is a poison."

"Nah!" Khadija replied, "some people just need to understand that it's not all about them."

Khadija bent down and fished the pledge out of Amina's pocket. She guessed that Amina would've found it useful as collateral to twist Anwar's arm in the event that he came between a mother and her children. But that was no more than speculation, and Khadija cared not. More important business was at hand, and needed to be concluded before the policemen started asking questions.

"The way I see it, you can leave this farm as a felon who attempted to murder her husband," Khadija told Amina, nudging the crowbar with her toe, "or you could let me, erm, help you spin an alternate reality."

Amina's eyes were wide open, but she just lay there. Bruno whimpered. He nudged Amina, but his concern still went unacknowledged.

"Don't worry," Khadija reassured the dog by nuzzling its nose, "you'll get what you need from her." Bruno licked Khadija's nose right back. They had learnt the gesture from Amina, and it was quite addictive.

Theirs was a world of uncertainty, and the woman lying on the floor was a key to navigating it. Amina was in that position because she relied on her marriage for a sense of security, but all things change, and there really was nothing to hold on to. Failing to admit that was why many people were deluded by all manner of fantasy, but even bandages couldn't cover the daunting lack of control that everyone suffered. Even magicians and dogs weren't exempt, and pure soul like Amina's was priceless to resolving their quest.

Amina's desperation to see her children again was an inalienable truth that she didn't really hate people at all. She actually loved them, as sharing her life with family made hers beautiful. Despite Amina's abrasive manner, it was her giving nature that finally shone through.

"If you trust me," Khadija told Amina, "you may even get to see your kids again."

It was unfortunately a situation in which Amina needed people, and Khadija took her tacit response as agreement. The crowbar was picked up and tossed into the thick bushes.

Bruno glanced at Khadija. He wasn't in the mood to play fetch at that ungodly hour.

Chapter Nine

His hands were weak, and it took an immense effort for Pa to push himself out of his chair. He managed to stand anyway, and smacked Brad across the cheek. Pa's catheter tumbled over. Brad reached out and caught the rod just before it hit the floor. He then carefully stood the device up for his dad again. His wife's reflexes weren't as sharp. Angelina's spoon dropped into her bowl and splashed soup all over her clothing. They were sitting around the dining table at Brad's home, and neither Angelina nor Brad dared to advise Pa that his already weak constitution would break if he didn't calm down. Brad wasn't only Pa's son. He was Pa's doctor too. In that moment though, anything he might've said would've been perceived as challenging Pa's authority. That was the level of respect that their culture entitled a patriarch to.

"I saw you!" Pa barked.

The pain in Brad's cheek reminded him of being disciplined by his father as a child but, now that Brad was older, he understood that Pa despised cowardice, and so, lifted his gaze bravely again.

"That bitch ruined the whole engagement, and now I'm on trial for it!" Brad grimaced. "Who the hell does she think she is?"

"That's not what I asked," Pa yelled back.

He didn't like his children using expletives, but let it slide this time. Pa wanted answers, in particular what Brad meant by Amina having taken matters into her own hands after they snuck behind the shed together at Leila's engagement.

"You did what?" Angelina gasped.

"Shut up and sit down!" Pa growled at her, "you'll get your turn when I leave."

"It wasn't like that at all," Brad remarked when Pa turned back to him. "Amina ambushed me…"

While his wife and father listened carefully, Brad admitted that it was indeed a quarrel that had transpired behind the shed on the morning of Leila's engagement. Amina had cornered him there to warn Brad to back off her husband, or else he was going to regret it. She didn't say how, and didn't give him a chance to speak either. Instead, Amina made herself perfectly clear that there were going to be repercussions if Brad didn't comply with her wishes.

"I told her to fuck off!" Brad whispered, knowing that his father didn't approve of cussing. Angrily, he continued anyway, "and that's probably why Amina ruined Leila's engagement!"

"You don't know that for sure," Pa replied, but Brad had an opinion of his own.

"Amina did it purposely…to prove a point," Brad said.

"And now Leila's heart is broken!" Angelina added. She was acknowledged, but not replied to.

"And while our daughter's marriage is in tatters, my brother is making a grab for the family inheritance," Brad sneered. "So, you tell me what you saw or heard behind the shed that morning?" Brad asked.

Hmm! Pa considered how to handle the request. Brad had painted himself as a victim, it seemed, to avoid discussing the actual tryst behind the shed. Pa reassured his son that he was interested in hearing Brad's side of the story, and that was all.

"Y'know, she teases me. She calls me 'Doctor Brad'..." he began.

That was how Amina lured Brad behind the shed that morning. Amina said that she needed help and, since both Amina and Anwar were so conscientiously applying themselves to their duties at Leila's engagement, Brad didn't refuse. Besides, Brad didn't suspect anything, as the brothers had set aside their differences for the day after Ma mediated a truce between them.

Once behind the shed however, Amina turned into another person entirely.

She went on a tirade that accused Brad of using her son to get a leg up on Anwar in their feud over the family inheritance. Brad was chastised for spreading rumours of Anwar's domestic violence as it unwittingly made Mo a casualty of sibling rivalry. When Brad argued that he had neither an intention to hurt Mo, nor was he responsible for Anwar beating his own son because of money, Amina went berserk.

"She wouldn't let me go until I agreed to apologize to her son," Brad said, "a little boy who doesn't understand what's going on!"

"Why didn't you?" Pa asked deadpan.

"Their domestic issues are not my problem!" Brad replied. "I've got bigger problems…like Leila being on the brink of divorce before she is even married."

"So, you're not having an affair with Amina?" Pa asked for clarification.

"What? …No!" Brad cried. "That woman is mad!"

He assured Pa, and his wife, that there was nothing sinister going on. Brad also pointed out that he had been dutifully treating Amina's little boy after Anwar beat Mo. It was action that determined true character, and not the diarrhoea of words that flew across social channels.

Amina, he opined, was someone who became difficult when she wasn't agreed with. She had a habit of hating people who crossed her, and had concocted a story in her head without ever having enquired as to Brad's perspective on the whole inheritance debacle.

"That's my professional medical opinion!" Brad exclaimed, sitting back in his chair and folding his arms.

"What happened then?" Pa asked.

"Eventually, she told me to back off, or else…" Brad said.

"And, did you agree?"

"I told you already," Brad said, "I told her to eff-off!"

"Good!" Angelina yelled, butting in. "It was Amina's idea that we wear those ridiculous leopard skin outfits!"

She was furious, but the scowl on Pa's face was enough to simmer her down. "I'm going to die soon," Pa told her, "I don't have the luxury of time."

"It's true," Brad said, supporting Angelina. "Amina enjoys making fools of others."

"You're just sour grapes about the engagement," Pa remarked, dismissing their insults.

"Maybe," Brad continued, "but I have nothing to lie about."

Pa believed him, until Brad made an unlikely appeal.

When Pa heard his son out, he recalled the effort it took to force himself out of bed, dress, and find an excuse that wouldn't raise Ma's suspicions as to why he was leaving the house in his condition. His driver was even forced to lie while corroborating Pa's story. All that just to end up wondering if it were better to donate the wealth that he had worked his entire life for to the pair of dogs in his backyard.

But Brad was determined to sell his point of view to Pa.

To him, it was pretty strange that Amina was teasing him for one minute, then angry at him for another, and perfectly focussed on her duties the next. He told Pa that perhaps it wasn't in the family's best interests to have someone as erratic as her sitting next to Anwar in the leadership seat.

"Anwar is very easily influenced," Brad said of his brother.

Pa smiled. Brad had obviously heard from Ma that the inheritance was offered to Anwar if he could prove himself, and now Brad felt the need to discredit his brother.

"What would you do instead?" Pa asked.

"An equal division of the inheritance so that everyone can manage their own affairs. It's fair," Brad replied.

Pa sat back in his chair. It wasn't an unreasonable suggestion, but was made perverse because of the motivation behind it. He took a long hard look at his son and realized that Brad had lost his way just as Anwar had. Despite all the wisdom of tradition that Pa had instilled in his sons as they grew up, they had both become greedy.

Brad then proved himself to be a true politician.

He asked Pa not to blame Amina as she seemed genuinely concerned about her children. In fact, Brad explained, that the altercation behind the shed proved her to be the only one who wasn't concerned about the money. Everyone else, including his own wife, were encouraging a fight that could present an advantage to their own lives.

"Imagine how I feel," Pa remarked. "Some things are more important than money," he said.

The colour suddenly drained from Brad's face. "That's what Amina said before she walked off from the shed," he remarked.

Back on the couch in the living room of his own home, Pa came clean about what was really bothering him. He asked Ma if they were such terrible parent's that their kids had turned out to be people who were completely opposite to who they were lovingly taught to be?

He had related the story of Brad's interrogation to add some perspective. The discovery that it was in fact Mo who had innocently hid a cricket in the barfi certainly did vindicate Amina of malice, but the engagement was ruined anyway.

"What if Amina knew, and allowed it to happen?" he asked Ma.

"To protect Mo?"

"Maybe she felt that Brad was a real threat to her family," Pa remarked.

"Amina could also have wanted to prove to Anwar that she was on his side," Ma thought out loud as it was clear that the kids were sleeping at their grandparents' because of tensions at their own home.

"Maybe she became rebellious because the Ebrahim's had angered her?"

"Amina is warm and witty, but never did handle rejection very well," Ma pondered.

"It's a bad attitude," Pa said, "but, sometimes, it's the only way to get attention."

"Why was she even feeling cast aside?" Ma sighed.

That, and many other questions, were left unanswered.

Neither Pa nor Ma could fathom the motivations for Amina's hearty laugh at the engagement, and they found themselves back where they started. None of these complications were the Ebrahim's business, but it now seemed like more negotiations were necessary to ensure that family politics wouldn't stymie the effort to make Leila smile again.

To clear the air once and for all, it was imperative that they had an account of the disastrous engagement from the horse's mouth before any conclusions were made. For the umpteenth time that night, they wondered where on earth Anwar and Amina were. Their mobile phones were unreachable, and no one else knew where they were. It was time to consider that something terrible had happened, and call the police for assistance.

"We can't possibly be such terrible parents, can we?" Ma asked.

"The truth is that each child is their own person," Pa said.

"Do you think we're being too controlling?" Ma asked.

"Do you think we have a choice?" Pa replied.

Chapter Ten

There was a time when that old farmhouse didn't sway in the heavy winds that blew across the plains surrounding it. Nor did it hunker in the eastern corner where it looked like the foundations had suffered a stroke. The pillars holding up the roof weren't standing askew, and the dishevelled grasses surrounding the plot were anything but an eyesore. In those days, Bruno recalled, the farmhouse was a home that stood tall and proud just as it did in the photograph hanging on the passage wall.

In it, he wore a pendant in place of a collar, and saw himself alongside the family he had shared the home with. The picture was taken aeons ago, but was still fresh in mind. The memory of it had never waned, for Bruno had held tightly onto it for just as long. His hope had finally manifested as the paean being sung outside by the howling winds of change. Bruno licked his lips and, instantly, the impression of him in the photograph ran its tongue across its mouth too.

The dog sauntered down the passage to the lounge.

There, the brown carpets, curtains and couches that oozed the stench of normality had been wished away by a spell, and the bare concrete shone a proud black just as any temple of ill-repute should. It was Bruno's original playground, and he traipsed across it to the fireplace where he stepped onto the hearth to push his paw into the cladding.

One brick moved, and then the entire mantlepiece shook to life. It grew out of the wall into a platform that stood upon pilasters at each end with the cornice hanging proudly at the facia. Bruno beheld the great edifice with reverence, and then hopped into the fire-hole. Moments later, he emerged upon the altar above. There he stood, surveying his kingdom.

"Ow-Ow-Owoooo!"

Mevlana chuckled from the temple floor below. The elder warlock sat on the floor with a pastel and mortar between his legs. In it he grinded salt, cloves, and remnants of burnt sage while Khadija planted candles in a circle, a foot apart from each other. The stage was almost set.

Bruno leapt off the mantlepiece and sailed across the air. He landed on an emblem painted with crushed bones and enamel in the centre of the magi's circle. He held his paw over the candle that stood there long enough to singe in the flame. Inspecting his wound brought him great satisfaction as it had passed the test.

"This time it'll work," Khadija remarked, smiling at him.

"Shut up!" Bruno barked back her. "I'll be the judge of that."

"I made a mistake the last time," Khadija mumbled. She stopped short of lighting the next candle, still cowered over it like a hunchback.

"Your error cost me my body," Bruno growled, and then stood upon his hind legs. "I'm a dog!"

"Trust me," Khadija pleaded, "M-M-Mother!"

"I trust no one!" Bruno sneered.

Between his legs was the disgusting appendage that hung from his pelvis. It had angered Bruno ever since he was forced to inhabit the abominable four-legged carcass people called a dog, but the time had arrived to transfer his soul into Amina's youthful and supple body. The very thought of being human again filled Bruno with ecstasy.

"If it goes wrong again, then we'll both be dogs!" Bruno cursed.

An uneasy pause followed, and then both mother and daughter shrieked with laughter. While Khadija's mother had been surviving as an animal, she and her mother had pined many a year to have their kinship restored to normal. It was now a possibility, and Bruno bared his teeth to mark its significance.

"There's a price to pay if you fail," he barked, "and it will last all of eternity."

Khadija's face instantly dropped. Her mother wasn't only the infamous black witch of Hekport, she was also moody as hell. Bruno knew that Khadija secretly enjoyed a sense of power for having his entire life in her hands, and he didn't want to encourage callousness. Khadija was a novice at magic, but there were no second chances in conducting the complicated spell Khadija had been tasked with. Years spent waiting to stumble upon the likes of Amina would be laid to waste.

"Don't disappoint me!" Bruno warned, reading Khadija's face for clues that fear had struck to the very heart of her. He then turned his attention to the body that was writhing across the temple floor.

"The pure soul…" Bruno taunted as he waltzed over to Amina.

She was gagged and bound, but still had spirit. That was good for the spell. Bruno needed Amina to be compos mentis. The deluge of emotions that would follow Amina's soul being discarded like a piece of used tissue paper would afford Bruno greater control over her body.

"Unfortunately, you won't ever see your kids again," Bruno told Amina, "but thank you for your contribution!"

It was apt to show gratitude to a fellow mother for Amina was a figure of utmost importance in her offspring's little lives. Every progeny has its roots in parentage, and ripping away the mainstay of their existence was traumatic to say the least. Bruno had noticed the impact of his transformation into a dog upon Khadija, so it was with a motherly instinct that he bit Amina's ankle and dragged her back to the centre of the sacred circle.

Mevlana sniggered.

His wife may have been a hairy dog, but she hadn't lost any of the cruelty she was famous for. He too couldn't wait for her to be returned to her former glory. They would all be a family again, and that old farmhouse would be a home again. It was the perfect way for them to begin wreaking havoc, just the way they had in the old days.

"Do you remember the time we swapped the husband and wife's voices?" he asked.

"Idiots!" Bruno replied, wagging his tail. "They actually believed that they were finishing each other's sentences!"

"He paid handsomely to be himself again," Mevlana laughed.

"You're good with money," Bruno remarked, looking around the house of dark magic that Mevlana had helped to establish themselves in.

While grinding herbs was the activity that Mevlana was presently engaged in, his powers extended far beyond rote magical administrations. He could command the elements, and could shift the earth upon which the farmhouse stood, so only those they had invited could find it. Often, he had brought inanimate objects to life. They would then be made gifts of, and given to unsuspecting people who the mystic wanted to spy on. Mevlana could also shape-shift, or disappear when he had to, but those were the old days, before Khadija misread a spell, and accidentally turned her mother into Bruno. Half of Mevlana's powers were also culled in the accident, and he was left as only a fraction of the warlock he used to be. Now he relied on an outdated grimoire to orchestrate his magic.

Mevlana slammed the book shut after processing the herbs. A small sample was carefully measured out with a spatula and flung into the air. The dust hung about, and finally settled on the dark temple floor, where it began twinkling like the coals of a hot fire.

Once they did their work, the floor shook, and Mevlana hopped back. The dangerous concoction brought a smile to his face, as the magical dust was functioning perfectly.

"Atta boy!" Bruno exclaimed.

Mevlana smiled, and patted the dog before carefully tipping the bowl of magical dust over into a little copper cauldron. Bruno instructed Khadija to take it to the altar, but Mevlana quickly referred back to the grimoire. He pointed out the instruction that recommended applying the dust to the temple floor instead.

"That's how the spell went wrong the last time" Bruno argued.

"No!" Mevlana refuted, his head still stuck in the spell book. "We failed to stick to the instructions." Mevlana didn't want to risk error again.

"Why do you have to throw your intelligence in my face every time?" Bruno growled.

"I'm the head of this coven!" Mevlana shouted, reacting to the dog's anger.

He was a tall man, and towered over the dog who stood only as high as all fours. The fabrication of the dust was his magical genius after all, and he demanded that the dog stop being difficult.

"Okay," Bruno conceded, and Mevlana relaxed. He backed down from the altercation, self-satisfied that his authority wasn't in question anymore.

"Why do you need it up there anyway?" he then asked to appease the situation.

"For this…" Bruno replied, putting his paw on the cauldron. When Mevlana took a closer look, Bruno tipped it over.

A minute amount of the magical dust was enough to scorch Mevlana's foot right off his body. But a lot more had spilt onto him, and Mevlana's limbs began instantly combusting. The dust sparkled prettily while eating through the flesh and bone of Mevlana's legs. He was cut down to stumps and, in a panic, slapped himself to stop the carnage at his thigh. He only succeeded in spreading the dust onto his hands though. Moments later, his fingers, wrist and arm had collapsed into ash.

Mevlana watched Bruno stand by as his chest disintegrated and his head rolled on the floor in disbelief. Suddenly it was Bruno who was towering above him.

"Why do you always have to be right?" Mevlana asked, while his own enchanted creation melting his eye.

"Because I am!" Bruno replied.

A heap of ash was all that was left on the cold stone floor where a husband and consort had stood before. Bruno wiped his paw in it to caress her husband for the last time, and then blew the ashes away.

Though once a powerful man, Bruno thought that Mevlana lacked vision. He hadn't fully understood that their daughter was the next generation of magical prowess. Through her, their waning powers would vicariously live on, and they would have been a family for much longer than Mevlana had ever imagined. Bruno wasn't going to allow Mevlana to jeopardize that. Sadly, Khadija's father was forced to take one for the team, but that was a mother's gift to her child.

"It's better to be useful than important," Bruno said.

Khadija gasped at having witnessed her mother murder her father. She didn't need to be told what next to do. She dutifully carried the copper cauldron over to the altar, just as Bruno expected. The faces who ordered her about may have changed, but she was still but a slave.

And though Amina was bound, she too watched in horror. She had never fathomed a family like this. They fed on each other like animals, and were mean to each other for such petty reasons that it begged the question as to how any family could stay together in the climate of so much rejection?

Perhaps the fear of losing a loved one far outweighed by the one of feeling completely alone.

Khadija now only had her mother. They were the only living souls left in their family. Running out of people to while away the days with inspired obedience in Khadija, and she opened the ancient grimoire up to a blank page. She swallowed a vile potion to see the secret words written there and, standing upon the temple's altar, Khadija bellowed out an incantation that invoked an unseen evil.

It was designed to deliver a child back into its mother's arms.

The temple turned murky, as if the candle-light had lost its exuberance. The sudden drop in temperature was a sign that indicated the spell had begun on a proper footing. This time the spell would work correctly, Khadija reassured herself. She then cut her palm open and squeezed a generous helping of her blood into a bowl. It was mixed with the revolting potion, and the entire concoction was gulped down. Moments later, Khadija was imbued with a green glow that served as a protective sheath. Bruno had insisted that Khadija wear it while doing the necessary evil.

He threw Khadija an affirmative nod from the witch's circle on the temple floor. Bruno was proud of her and, if everything went according to plan, he would be human again. Anticipation filled him, for both his transformation, and Khadija's victory. A mother was about to watch a child ascend to her rightful station in life.

Khadija's eyes rolled over and turned white. She dipped a sacred ladle into the copper cauldron and scattered a heap of the magical dust across the temple floor. The sprinklings landed hither-tither, where they burst into flames, and dissolved into the temple floor. The concrete lost its durability, and rippled as a body of water does. Over and over, Khadija chanted an ancient hex that spun the temple floor, and sent it draining away into a dark vortex.

The void left behind was cold and intimidating.

Amina stared into it from the witch's circle. It was the only part of the temple floor that hadn't disappeared into the abyss. Candles lit its perimeter, and it floated magically above the chasm with neither strings nor support. Peering over the edge, Amina was hypnotized. The sight of the cosmic hole alone produced a dizzy spell that overcame her, and she lost her balance. She tipped over the edge of the witch's circle, and fell right into empty void.

A claw suddenly dug into her shoulder, and Bruno dragged her back up to safety. He didn't want Amina to miss the main attraction.

Another ladle of the mystical dust was poured into the dark void and, in the nowhere below, a fire erupted. Just as spontaneously, it extinguished itself. In its place, flowered a glowing white ball.

It was a dimensional door that peeped, like a window, into the quiet cosmos beyond. There, time was no more, and everything that had ever existed was still inimitably alive behind the veil of ordinary perception. Thousands of renditions of everything that was, is, and still to come, made a mesmerizing spectrum of colour. There were no boundaries in sight, and therefore no centre to discern. It was the fabric of life, in its rawest form.

"Magnificent isn't it?" Bruno asked with the myriad of colours reflecting in his eyes.

"I've always felt it!" Amina gasped. Indeed, there was a strange familiarity to it, as if those same colours painted the ebbs and flows of her life.

For the first time Amina felt a sense of true connection within, and all the relationships she sought through others had only been a substitute. She had been carrying this gift within herself all along as a sense that she was, in actuality, a part of something much larger.

When Khadija finished reciting her incantation, a dark patch along the evocative range of creation moved. It turned into a wisp of smoke, and rose steadily through the dimensional doorway to settle as a dense fog about the temple.

It stank horribly, and Bruno took a deep sniff of it before crouching over and defecating. Any witch worth her salt knew that the only way to gain a demon's trust was to assimilate it, and so Bruno nibbled at his own hot and steamy mess. At first, a sense of curiosity seemed to permeate the fog, and two eyes of scorching violet materialized, blinking with interest. Bruno licked some more. The dark smog then gained the definition of a menacing creature.

With those eyes, it examined Bruno from snout to tail. It spun around his torso, and met him vis-à-vis once again. Bruno opened his jaw and, with a deafening thud, the creature vanished into his mouth. Moments later, it emerged from the dog's gullet pulling a delicate golden thread. It glowed so beautifully that Amina gasped, and that was what the creature was hovering about for. It entered her with the cord, pulling it down her throat.

Somewhere deep within, Amina felt herself stirring.

It was a queasy feeling to be invaded by the witch's soul. Each time the golden thread throbbed inside Amina, she felt herself diminished in some way, and her consciousness began waning. As Amina shrunk within, the panic of being a prisoner in her own body became an abrupt reality.

The sound of cymbals crashing rumbled in the temple. "Do everything twice!" Khadija shouted from the altar, and the noise echoed again. Bruno sniggered as a horrible melody began reverberating in the empty space.

"Submit yourself to me," he advised. Having been trapped in a dog's body for what seemed forever, Bruno knew how excruciating a loss of freedom was. "Submit yourself to me, and I won't torture you."

"Why should I trust you?" Amina sneered.

"We're going to be together inside your body for a long time," Bruno replied, "why make things difficult?"

"You don't own me," Amina cried. "No one does!"

"Oh, pure soul…" Bruno sang, "taking the moral high ground will only make you suffer."

"I'm just too tired of people using me."

Bruno laughed. "You have it all wrong," he explained, "you decide who to put first in your life."

Though Amina loved animals, she wasn't used to taking advice from dogs. But Bruno made sense, and his offer now seemed like a generous one. It came from a mother who was securing the future of her daughter, and that was exactly what Amina had done for her son while enduring everything she had that night. One mother cannot expect her child to be more precious than another's.

Amina's heart sank. Her disapproval really meant nothing in actual fact, and that was the healthy cynicism with which she decided that there was nothing else to live for.

Amina whispered her eulogy into the ether. It was her final wish. Her estranged body would soon be walking around with someone else inside it. Unable to be present for her children anymore, Amina hoped they wouldn't grow up feeling betrayed or abandoned by their mother. Instead, she gave Mo and Fati the gift of freedom that she was about to lose. Amina wished that every memory of her vanished from their minds, and her children forgot her.

Perhaps her desire was act of courage, but it was also the moment of weakness in which Amina agreed to Bruno's bargain and submitted to the dog. She allowed herself to become his possession, as being useful to her children was the only logic left to consider.

Life drained away from Amina's eyes as a new soul took residency within her. Bruno watched her make the sacrifice, saddened by the thought of a bond between a mother and her children being severed. But the spell was working, and the yearning to hold Khadija again was strong.

And, while Amina was being conquered by the wicked witch of Hekport in the temple above, in the basement below the farmhouse a little pinkie finger stood crooked no more.

Anwar examined his hand in a beam of light that streamed into the dark cellar. He was standing before the only window he could find. His finger was swollen, but the pain was bearable. The bigger problem was himself. He was too large to climb through the tiny window, and escape the basement. Anwar grimaced. He was angry at himself for other reasons already.

The words 'if only you knew' kept playing in his mind.

Anwar just couldn't figure out what Amina had meant by them. They were obviously significant because she had said them as a substitute to smashing his face in with a crowbar. Suspicion, however, were disease that Anwar couldn't afford to catch if he was to retrieve the pledge that would surely ruin his life. He had written it under duress, and only a little window now stood between him and finding Amina. That was the priority.

Scratching around in the black, however, sent Anwar tumbling over. He knocked his knee painfully against a solid object, and went limp in one leg. The agony drove him on to find the crowbar that Amina had wielded before. Anwar thought it would be useful to smash through the window and claw his way out of the cellar, but his blind determination only managed to trip himself up over another hidden thing. He found his pants damp with his own blood, and finally stopped to breathe.

Anger was useless to navigate the darkness.

With common sense fuelling his actions instead, Anwar's luck turned. He stumbled upon a monkey wrench, which smashed the glass effortlessly. Anwar then heaved himself up using a box to stand on. His head stuck through the window-frame easily enough, but squeezing the rest of himself through the tiny gap still seemed impossible.

It took a little ingenuity and lot of twisting this way and that before Anwar dragged himself, inch by inch, through the little window. Needless to say, it was a painful experience, but he just got on with it. Shards of glass cut through his hands and legs until Anwar emerged into the sullen but free night. Having conquered the infinitesimally small rectangle in the wall, a deep breath of fresh air was in order, and Anwar stood up a new man. Ah!

Freedom helped Anwar understand how persecuted Amina may have felt while dealing with the pressures of the engagement debacle. He was especially hard on her too. As Amina's closest ally, Anwar hardly offered her any support while so mesmerized by the cold-hard cash that his inheritance promised. While he had previously justified riches as a worthwhile pursuit in the name of his family's well-being, Anwar now had a change of mind. All his greed had accomplished was to drive a wedge between him and the family that he loved.

Lightning flashed in the sky. Suddenly, Anwar wasn't driven to retrieve the pledge he had written anymore. On his lips was single word: Amina! Back in the city, his children were waiting for their mother.

His escape from the basement however was not unanimously taken as a victory. When

Anwar spun around, he found himself standing face-to-face with the grape-eyed farmhand and his pack of dogs. They had been waiting for him rather patiently, and ambushed Anwar with his back up against the wall. The dogs growled and the farmhand bared his teeth.

"Sit!" Anwar instinctively said.

The word just fell out of his mouth. It felt right though, so Anwar followed through by lowering his palms toward the ground. He was hopeful that a distraction would buy some time to make a run for it, or use the monkey wrench to stave the dogs off, but he was not expecting the canines to actually obey him. Even more surprising was that the grape-eyed farmhand was equally obedient. He too followed Anwar's palms and squatted alongside the animals. The entourage of killer dogs stopped growling once their master was subdued. They all just sat there, eagerly awaiting further instructions.

"Stay!" Anwar said more confidently.

It seemed a reasonable suggestion to follow-up with. To his surprise, the farmhand and his dogs submitted once again while Anwar slowly sidled away.

He stepped backwards, until reaching the corner of the house, and then ran off. A safe distance away, Anwar stopped and flung himself against the wall to catch his breath. Phew! Miraculous as it was that those dogs had obeyed him, Anwar laughed, he really had no idea why they actually had.

He looked at his hands. They seemed to shimmer, and Anwar wondered how he had lived for all his years without having yet understood his own power.

It struck Anwar that the physique he had spent so much time in the gym sculpting still didn't substitute for simply acknowledging himself. It was his own insecurities that had eroded his trust in Amina, and had made a control freak of him. What he needed was an understanding of himself, for it begot respect, which then flowered into trust.

That was the magic in his and Amina's marriage. The respect was mutual until recently.

The call to mend their relationship came when light flashed in a window nearby. Anwar tightened his grip on the monkey wrench, and stepped up as the husband he was meant to be.

What good a tool would do in a witch's coven was dubious though. It was, however, the only weapon Anwar had to face the evil that was underway in the farmhouse's lounge. It,

Anwar noticed when climbing through the window, had undergone a drastic remodelling. He preferred the brown colour scheme, in all honesty, and it wasn't ideal either to have found Amina kneeling on a floating platform with a golden snake in her mouth.

Anwar attempted to leap across to her, but quickly scrambled back up to the windowsill. There was no floor beneath his feet, and the void would've swallowed him whole had he jumped. A fat load of good that would've done.

"Amina!" he shouted.

"Arrgh!" Bruno barked. It seemed that no one was ever happy when things went his way. It really was a dog's life he was living.

"Go away!" Amina yelled back.

"Don't be stubborn," Anwar shouted at his wife.

"Don't tell me what to do!" she cried right back, but then bit her lip. Those words were ridiculous in these circumstances.

Sensible as Amina was, her own intelligence sometimes didn't serve her well. She understood finally that her episodes were really just that, allowing the noise in her head to overwhelm her to such an extent that she confused herself. There was no need, however, to believe all the stories that were concocted in her head, and Amina recognized her circumstances for what they were. Danger was an apt word for it.

"Help!" she shouted. Trying to prove a point was thing of the past.

Anwar weighed the monkey wrench in his hand. He tied it to his belt-buckle, and then swung the strip of leather over the lounge's curtain rail. A firm tug on the loop bent it, and Anwar skied along the wall, down the length of the rod. At the end, he flung himself as hard as he could toward the temple's altar. A noble effort it was, and Amina watched with relief as the monkey wrench fell into the abyss instead of her husband.

She lost track of Anwar though when accosted by a blinding light.

The golden cord between herself and Bruno began throbbing brighter than ever before. It pulled taut, and yanked Bruno up upon his paws. The cord reeled the dog in, one step at a time. With the first, Bruno's snout withered into a nose, and his ears shrunk into the side of his head. The next step forward transformed the dog's torso into that of a woman's. Like a faun, half animal and half human, Bruno was then drawn yet another step closer to Amina. His four legs melted into two, and upon them Bruno stood up as the translucent effigy of a fully-formed human being.

"You're the woman in the picture!" Amina gasped.

She was looking at the wicked witch of Hekport right in the eye. Khadija's mother was instantly recognizable from the photograph that Amina had seen on the passage wall. There was but a step between the two women, and the claustrophobia was unbearable.

Anwar didn't know any magic, but he did know how to fight. He leapt into the fire hole in the hearth, and surprised Khadija up on the altar. Her white and vacant eyes frightened him, but he bravely threw himself upon the witch nevertheless. It was the first time Anwar had fought a woman with his hands, and managed to push her away from the grimoire, but no brute could penetrate the protective green sheath around Khadija.

With Khadija's attention diverted though, the spell stalled.

The golden cord between Amina and the phantom witch went limp. The wicked witch of Hekport tried to maintain her footing by pulling on the cord, but still regressed a step, and fell upon all fours again. Yelling instructions to Khadija proved to be an effort in vain as the words of an apparition were not yet of this world, and only produced silence when spoken.

Without guidance from her mother, Khadija was left to her own devices. It was an opportunity to prove her worth, and she seized the moment by grabbing the copper cauldron. Khadija swung it at Anwar, scattering the magical dust. The cloud hung in the air between them while Anwar smiled confidently. To him, it looked harmless, and he dove right through it.

To his horror, Anwar found his clothing and hair being scorched away as he fell to the floor, writhing in pain. Khadija shrieked with laughter before turning her attention back to the grimoire. Moments later, the spell was resumed, and Khadija's mother stepped up to Amina, proudly standing on two legs again.

Behind Khadija though, a flaming man rose to his feet. It was the last act of chivalry that Anwar could afford, but there were two children out there waiting to be fetched by their parents.

He pounced upon Khadija with what was left of him. It didn't end well though when Khadija managed to step out of the way, just in time, and Anwar landed on his face. His ashes scattered across the altar while Khadija jeered, and Amina gasped. But Anwar stood up with grimoire in his hand. He had landed right on top of it. It too had caught alight in his flaming hands, and he flung the book into the void.

Everything was suddenly reversed.

The green glow around Khadija dissolved, and her protective sheath disappeared. Her eyes rolled around in their sockets, the pupils taking a moment to focus on what had just happened. The furious dust that consumed Anwar lost its potency, and his wounds were miraculously restored to full health. The golden cord snapped, and the wicked witch of Hekport collapsed upon all fours. Her torso grew a carpet of hair, and Khadija's mother was trapped once again in Bruno's body. The smog demon then vanished, and the temple was left a wreck.

The spell had once again gone awry.

Anwar pushed Khadija aside, and leapt off the altar. He ran his legs through the air as he sailed across to the witch's circle and landed on the floating disk. Anwar hurried over to Amina, who had collapsed from exhaustion. Hurriedly, he untied her, and set Amina free.

"No one leaves you hanging in the middle of nowhere," he said.

Amina threw her arms around Anwar. "What was I thinking trying to destroy you?" she whispered.

"Amina!" Anwar smiled, "I like saying your name!"

"And I love looking at your face" she replied.

She leaned in to nibble at Anwar's nose, and he bit hers lightly in return. They belonged to each other.

Romance however didn't have much of a place in a witch's circle. With his hopes of being human fast draining away, Bruno bared his teeth and growled. He was ready to rip the lovers apart, and would have if not distracted by a dull thud. By the time Bruno chased his tail, it was too late. Khadija's jaw was gaping, and her mouth stood wide open. The violet eyes of the smoky demon narrowed at the invitation, and it dove into her mouth. So desperate was Khadija to see her mother again that she sold her soul to the demon.

"Do everything twice!" Khadija growled in a gruff voice.

Khadija then disintegrated into a dark smog that infected the temple with confusion. Amina and Anwar held tightly onto each other while the evil haze pushed them toward the edge of the witch's circle. One misstep and they both would tumble into the abyss.

"I'll handle this," Anwar said, pushing Amina behind him.

"Do you even know what you're doing?"
Amina asked. It was such disagreements that
had brought them to the farmhouse in the
first place.

"Now's really not the time for a
communication problem!" Anwar yelled.

"Then let's trust each other," Amina
whispered, holding Anwar's hand.

They came together as they were. It was the
only way they could be. Standing beside each
other, there was nothing else to do but grab
Bruno. Anwar held the dog tightly, and Amina
threw her arms around them to secure Bruno.
What looked like a group hug was actually a
standoff in which Bruno was their hostage,
and Anwar threatened to throw the dog into
the void below.

A golden thread suddenly appeared and
lassoed the lot of them, but Khadija was no
pure soul and the demon rejected her. It

puffed out like a dusty carpet being hit with a stick, and in its wake was left Khadija's discarded body. There she lay, trembling in the centre of the witch's circle, spent.

The demon returned to the netherworld, slamming the dimensional doorway shut behind it. The vortex stopped spinning, and the temple floor returned to its usually solid consistency. The eerie music that echoed in the temple halted with two crashes of a cymbal, and the attack was abated. Anwar regained a safe footing for himself and Amina, and silence befell them all.

All that could be heard was a soft and relentless sobbing.

Anwar and Amina were too shocked to shed a tear, and dogs weren't known to have sad spells. It was Khadija who was sad. The opportunity to be reunited with her mother was completely lost. She was a disappointment to Bruno, and was damned to loneliness for aeons to come.

"She needs me," Bruno whispered pitifully, and Amina understood the plight of a mother. Amina loosened her grip, and Anwar lowered the dog gently to the floor.

Bruno crept up to Khadija and licked her cheek, but she continued to lay there with a broken heart.

"Ow-Ow-Owoooo!" Bruno howled, sharing in Khadija's pain.

That was all that they could share.

Chapter Eleven

The car swerved dangerously in the loose
sand. Anwar put his foot down anyway, and
steered back onto the dusty path that led away
from the farmhouse, past the gate at the
perimeter, and yonder. Beyond Hekport was
the world that he and Amina were familiar
with, where their children and family were
waiting for them. Dirt clouds billowed behind
them and, through the rear windscreen,
Amina watched the old farmhouse shrink in
the distance. The night that they had spent
there was now no more than the past.

Out of it came a black dog running at full
speed. It pushed forward upon its hind legs,
catching up to the car. Bruno's tongue flapped
wildly in the wind and, when Amina heard his

desperate barking, she wound her window down. Above the din of the roaring engine, she could scarcely hear a word of what Bruno was saying. It sounded like he was asking for forgiveness.

The car suddenly swerved and ran the dog over.

"What the hell are you doing?" Amina yelled, twisting around in her seat.

Khadija was laying on the backseat in the same position that Amina had put her there. Her eyes were wide open, staring at the open skies through the windshield.

"Why did you bring her?" Anwar asked.

"She needs help," Amina replied.

Anwar remained focussed on the road, tightening his grip on the steering wheel. His foot was flat on the pedal, and perhaps he was locked in a mental episode that brought on a lapse of judgement. Amina gently caressed his arm. She assured him that the past was certainly not the future. An awareness of what they were doing was all they needed. Their lives were in their own hands and, to prove it, she folded the pledge that Anwar had written and put it safely in her pocket. Anwar eased up, and Amina could tell that he was receptive again.

As for Khadija, remaining in a home that had festered with regretful memories was not a life for young woman to be living. Amina took pity on Khadija, which was why she invited her to leave the farm with them. In a strange way, Amina was thankful to Khadija. The witchlet had helped Amina to realize how far she was willing to go for her beloved ones.

"We'll take her to Pa," Amina told Anwar, swinging back around in her seat. "Maybe this feud with Brad needs some practical magic."

Anwar liked the sound of that. He dropped a gear, and the car jerked forward. Amina fastened her seatbelt as they smashed through the gate at the perimeter of the ranch, and flew past the grape-eyed farmhand and his dogs. On the road out of Hekport, Anwar didn't give a damn about his car anymore. All he needed was sitting right next to him.

And outside Amina's window, the navy night sky had turned rose and yellow. A new day was dawning. As the sun crept up over the horizon, its rays shot across the countryside, and everything was imbued with a golden glow. The stony crags looked like ancient sages, the farmstall seemed a refreshing stop, and the road sign that read 'Hekport' once again stood out uninvitingly as a place that no one wanted to visit.

When they got to the end of the dusty path, Anwar swerved onto the road that led back home. The silhouette of their car dissolved into the rising sun, but the roar of the engines could still be heard for miles and miles.

It would only stop once Amina had her children in her arms again.

Across town, the clock on the wall kept ticking away relentlessly. The hands had been turning one anxious second at a time. It hypnotized both Ma and Pa into fearing the worst. With dawn breaking, it was easy to presume that some catastrophe had befallen Anwar and Amina during the night. It was time to call for help, though there was some trepidation to as Pa had a nagging feeling that it was about to come to them.

"Who was this woman on the farm?" Ma asked.

"Someone who helps people," Pa replied.

"Helps people?"

"Y'know, the type of help you need when you don't know what to do," Pa said after taking a breath of oxygen from the mask. He returned it to the tank.

"Well, we were having a tough time back then," Ma observed, "Anwar and Brad were still kids." It was a time when their sons weren't fighting over their father's inheritance because Pa had nothing to his name.

"After that visit, everything changed," Pa explained.

"What did she do?"

"I'm not even sure," Pa replied, "I was given something to drink, and I became a wealthy man thereafter with no special effort on my part."

"I don't understand. What did she want in return for your fortune?" Ma asked.

"Nothing!" Pa replied.

"Nothing?"

"The woman said that a time will come," he said.

"That's it?"

"I assumed that it was a time to repay the debt," Pa remarked.

"How would you know when?" Ma asked.

"She said that someone would be sent to me," Pa replied, getting pensive about what that meant too.

"Hmm!" Ma remarked, "maybe you're just questioning things, the way people do when they're…" Ma said, but cut her words due to a tear welling-up in her eye. Pa held her hand. He knew what she meant. His illness was consuming him day by day.

"That's just it," Pa explained, "I can't die with that debt still hanging over my head. I won't."

It was his cross to bear. The wealth that had so instantly come to him after seeing the woman on the farm had led to a wonderful life with his family, but the same money was now responsible for the malcontent that was tearing them apart.

As a patriarch, Pa had for many years simply issued an instruction for his family to love one other to develop a support system between them, but it was obvious now that discipline didn't replace trust. It couldn't. They were two different things. Trust wasn't implicit, and couldn't be transferred. Even the closest family members had to listen to and understand each other to truly foster a kinship, or else the patriarchal values that Pa had crooned for so long only reduced the members of his beloved family to objects.

A change was needed if Pa didn't want greed to poison the future generations of his family.

Pa resolved to entertain the progressive ideas that his sons were offering to settle the inheritance feud. It departed from tradition, yes, but time marched on, and progress was the only creature that was never ever fully formed. Thankfully too, as embracing change rendered Pa trustworthy enough to service his debt when the time to settle it finally came. Practically, it was all that he could do to avoid transferring his debt to his children.

Beyond that, people could only be trusted to be themselves.

Every person was a world unto their own, and it was impossible to tell what the climate in the privacy of another's mind was. Trust then had to be demonstrated through action.

Ma held Pa's hand, then smiled.

"So, I guess I win!" she exclaimed.

"No!" Pa retorted.

"Yes!" Ma said. "The feud over the inheritance is a perfect example of people excluding each other for selfish reasons, and that eroded trust."

"That wasn't the wager!" Pa replied, "and this experiment hasn't failed just yet."

"It has too, and that was the wager," Ma reminded him. "You bet that an adherence to good values would foster respect between people, and then they would trust each other."

"C'mon!" Pa argued, "Amina protected her son in such a way that his life was shaped in ways Mo will never even know."

"Yes, but it came from within Amina, not from any imposed morality," Ma said. "Remember, she wasn't taught to rebel against the family."

"Hmm! …I guess that what comes from within a human being is purer than any teaching."

"Then you admit that this has been a failed experiment!" Ma exclaimed.

Pa sighed. "I have an idea!" he said after scratching his beard for a few moments. "Let's scrap this experiment and start a new family?"

"What did you have in mind?"

"We'll only keep little Mo and his sister," Pa explained, "we'll call him Adam, and her, Eve."

"Hmm, two fresh souls…" Ma observed. "Well, this time, I'm choosing where it happens," she said, "I've always dreamt of a world in the clouds."

"Your head is always in the clouds!" Pa remarked.

The End.

I hope you enjoyed this story. Please review this title on my website, GoodReads, or the bookstore you purchased from. Feedback helps me write more of the stories you like.

Find my books on Amazon, Smashwords, Kobo, the iStore, and many libraries. Or stay updated on new books, artworks, and creative products by signing up to my newsletter at:

whiteteastudios.com

Connect with Me

Twitter: @yousuftilly

Facebook: facebook.com/whiteteastudios

Website: whiteteastudios.com

More by Yousuf Tilly

TRAVEL – SPIRITUALITY. IN PRINT OR EBOOK AT:

Amazon, Apple, Kobo, Smashwords, Scribd, and many libraries.

DEARLY BELOVED

30 Days in the Osho Ashram, Discovering the Soul of a Spiritual Enterprise.

Rebellious Spirits from all over the world attend the 'Work as Meditation' programme at the OSHO ashram in India. They go there to cultivate the meditative skills that help to understand why they are not the people they intend to be, but the heavy-hand with which the commune is governed seeks its own goals, and between the two are the differences that clarify spiritual guidance from clever entrepreneurship.

This travel adventure explores the inner-workings of the ashram established by the notorious Bhagwan Shree Rajneesh, also known as Osho, who coined 'fuck' as the most magical word in the English language. Google it!

In *Dearly Beloved* you'll experience his wacky meditations, have those deep spiritual conversations reserved for late nights beneath the stars, and meet those who have learnt to dance to the rhythm of life.

Jump in, you may discover who you are!

Readers Say:

"Absolutely loving it!" "Love the style!" "The descriptions made me feel like I was right there!" "Concise, precise and thoroughly entertaining!"

Read a sample chapter now:

https://whiteteastudios.com/books/

AN UNEXPECTED JOURNEY. AN UNEXPECTED LOVE.

COME BACK ABAYOMI

YOUSUF TILLY

* WINNER: DEPT. ARTS & CULTURE PUBLISHING GRANT *

THRILLER – ROMANCE. IN PRINT OR EBOOK AT:

Amazon, Apple, Kobo, Smashwords, Scribd, and many libraries.

COME BACK ABAYOMI

An Unexpected Journey. An Unexpected Love.

High-powered attorney at law, Abayomi, is still an authentic African woman. She's invited to South Africa on a diplomatic mission, then gets abducted in a surprise xenophobic attack!

In a travel adventure through historic Johannesburg, Abayomi finds herself tangled in an unfolding conspiracy of political big-wigs, priests and immigrant children. Then again, she's dangerously drawn to her kidnapper when she senses a man beneath the beast. To trust her instincts or not, that's the journey of a capable woman challenging male dominance.

Readers Say:
"The unspoken passion is a winner." "Abayomi is big enough to say this is who I am." "He's aloof and mysterious, the type of guy who wants to do good but doesn't know how." "A suspenseful book with interesting characters and an authentic African feel." - More reviews online.

Read two sample chapters now:
https://whiteteastudios.com/books/

326

PARANORMAL – THRILLER – TRUE STORY. IN PRINT OR EBOOK AT:

Amazon, Apple, Kobo, Smashwords, Scribd, and many libraries.

BAD LOVE

Who do you sleep with?

When the universe shifts, a young writer struggling to express himself suddenly drops into the magical world of an exorcist. He finds himself pinning down a frail woman with five men and, while wondering what the hell he's doing, comes face to face with the devil possessing her. As the clues to exorcise her unfold, dark family secrets come to light, and the writer questions whether people are worse than the devil?

Readers Say:

"First I thought it was a joke, then..." "Didn't see that coming!" "I was spellbound, pun intended!" "Loved this story...I want more!" "Came back to re-read this story numerous times."

Read it online now: https://whiteteastudios.com/books/